The Enchanted Cruise

A *novel* by

LAURA MCCRACKEN

Kindle Books 2022

Second Edition

For my children Grace and Sam,
who inspired this book
and for all children who love an adventure.

With many thanks to
my Mum and Dad
for their endless encouragement.
To my husband and brother
for their endless support.

Table of Contents

Chapter 1

The Smell of the Sea

"Grace! Sam! Time to go." shouted Mom.

Grace and Sam slowly made their way down the stairs. They were not in any rush. Mom bombarded them with questions. They were always the same questions, the ones which seemed to have been asked every time they left the house, for as long as they could remember. It did not seem to matter if they were heading to a friend's house, off to school, or like today, going on vacation.

Mom always had at least four demands: "Have you brushed your teeth?" "Have you been to the bathroom?", "Where are your shoes?" , "Have you seen the car keys?" Grace rolled her eyes at Sam who giggled. "Have you been to the bathroom?" *Really*, thought Sam, *they were not two years old anymore. Grace was nearly 13 Sam was 10 - No need for the potty training reminders!* There was no telling Mom though. Grace was thinking the same, she was sure that on her wedding day her Mom would ask the same questions.

Luckily, Mom was so occupied with her own pre-leave-the-house preparations that she did not notice the children's eye rolling or giggling at her expense.

Soon Grace and Sam were no longer barefoot but were outside on the driveway, hoping to avoid any more questions from Mom. Mom, of course, was still busy bustling around fussing over

Molly, the cat and hastily scribbling on the note of instructions for the cat sitter and partaking in various other last minute events, that in reality had already been done. It would be at least ten minutes until she was ready. So the children dutifully, if not a little sullenly, got into the car.

Dad was also patiently waiting outside for Mom, pretending to rearrange the luggage and glancing on occasion at his watch. As the kids fastened their seat belts, he climbed in the driver's seat. "Are you ready for an adventure?" Dad said, "You two are going to love being at sea." Again both kids rolled their eyes.

Grace and Sam were sure that they would not enjoy this vacation one bit. They were heading to the port an hour away to go on the cruise, which Dad had booked for Mom to celebrate their 15th wedding anniversary.

The kids had been shown the brochure for the 'Prestige cruise line' before Mom and Dad had booked the cruise. They had desperately tried to persuade them to choose a Ponder cruise. Ponder cruises were awesome for a number of reasons and the kids could quote all the reasons of awesomeness by heart. The Ponder cruises have various celebrity characters from their favorite show walking around handing out free merchandise, they have four pools, one with three huge water slides, and a zip-line that goes right over the dining hall. There is a twenty-four hour free video game center, free high speed Wi-Fi in all rooms and evening firework displays.

Grace and Sam's friend, Luca, had been on a Ponder Cruise during the school spring break. The children had been to Luca's house when he returned. Luca's Dad had shown them pictures of their trip. There were photos of Luca jet skiing, waterskiing, watching the seal show, on the rope course around the top deck, in the twenty four hour cupcake building factory, sampling the fifty two flavors of ice cream, and watching the evening firework display by a fire pit where they were roasting s'mores.

But that was Ponder cruise line - they were not going on that one. Prestige Cruise Line had nothing like the 'awesome' list of excitement that Luca's cruise had to offer. Instead, Prestige Cruise's brochure claimed it had a guarantee that each guest would have an available deckchair. They offered free pilates on the deck in the morning, cribbage classes in the afternoon in the 'Moonlight lounge', gourmet French cooking lessons every second day and 'memory foam' mattresses on the beds.

Grace and Sam were not sure what exactly 'cribbage' was, or how 'gourmet cooking' differed from 'normal cooking' but they were pretty sure these were things that older people liked and certainly not as exciting as water skiing or rope climbing. Sam had been sort of excited about the memory foam mattress until Grace had told him this was not a mattress with a real memory (Sam loves gadgets) but a type of mattress which in Grace's words, "old people prefer". They remembered thinking then: *This does not look good.*

Why were they choosing Prestige for their cruise? Well, basically, when Mom told Dad she wanted to go on a cruise, Dad had researched every cruise line online. He had painstakingly researched them for their safety and hygiene standards. Prestige Cruise Line had come up tops for the last two years. Sam had explained of course it would come up better than Ponder on safety and hygiene - Prestige did not have jet skiing or ropes courses and of course the cupcake station and ice cream nook were bound to get a little messy on occasion. But the Prestige it was.

Grace had also tried hard to convince Mom and Dad to change their mind. She argued that Mom and Dad would have a much better time, if she and Sam were busy and not under their feet all the time. She had even researched on the internet which cruise had come up tops for kid's activities. In case you were wondering, Ponder Cruise has been tops for the last 5 years.

Grace had been so desperate that she had gone so far as to put on a powerpoint presentation about what Ponder had to offer in comparison to Prestige. (Grace was great at computers. She had been putting every family debate into powerpoint presentations ever since her third grade class did a powerpoint presentation on Rocks and Minerals).

Sam pleaded, saying he would mow the lawn for free and pick up everything he dropped for two weeks if his parents would change their mind and switch to Ponder. This did not work as Mom reminded him mowing the lawn was on his chore list anyway. Plus, he should always pick up his belongings. *Too bad*, Sam had said resignedly.

Grace eventually had finally and extremely begrudgingly come to the conclusion that despite the fact she thought her 4 minute 35 second presentation on "Cruise Comparisons" was worthy of a high schooler, their parents would never be convinced. For their parents the entertainment/fun factor awards were worth a lot less than a safe and clean cruise. Grace had considered another slide show, but Sam claimed even he, who regularly watched YouTube presentations on how to wear beanie hats, was bored of 'presentations'. So it was all over when the tickets arrived in the post. The family vacation was going to be a Prestige cruise. The Ship was named 'The Brilldom', or as Grace and Sam secretly had renamed it "The Boredom".

Roll on a month to summer vacation and there they were waiting in the car for Mom, bags packed and ready for a week of boredom on 'The Boredom'. Sam sighed and powered on his Ipod to listen to some rap music. Grace also sighed and promised herself, *When I am a parent I will always choose what is more fun for the kids, over any other alternative.*

Finally Mom came out, sat down huffing and puffing and immediately started complaining that they were going to be late and that they were always late. It was Dad's time to sigh! The engine started, Mom stopped complaining and they were off.

An hour later, they were at the dock in a large line of cars waiting to find a parking spot at the cruise line's car park.

They rolled down their windows and smelt the sea.

Chapter Two

Embarkation

'Embarkation', Grace and Sam found out, is a big word meaning - getting onto the ship. Grace and Sam also soon found out that embarkation is not fun, not easy and certainly not quick. There were a ton of people all wandering around looking lost.

Lines of people in all directions, lines to give in your luggage, lines to show your documents, lines to go through security, lines to show your passports and lines to get in a line to get to the line to get on the ship. It was super hot, crowded and each line seemed to take longer than the other. There was no way to speed it up. They were trapped.

Sam made himself laugh "I guess this is what they mean when they talk about a 'cruise line'," he commented. "Cruise-line. Hahaha, get it a cruise with lines!" Mom and Dad did not find it quite as amusing but Grace saw his humor. Still she thought the line was depressingly long, slow and hot.

In between the luggage line and the document line there was a big hall of tables. At the tables sat members of the cruise staff advertising events and clubs. Sure enough there was the cribbage club, the gourmet cook with a white chef's hat and large black beard advertising cooking classes and a rather scary looking gym instructor advertising pilates classes. The gym instructor was particularly notable. He had bright, bronze colored skin and he was flexing his muscles and wearing very short, white shorts. His hair was perfectly greased back into a ponytail. They continued walking through the hall and passed a couple more tables of bored looking staff members advertising crossword clubs, puzzle evenings, French and Italian courses. Nothing appealed to the children.

They passed the Gym instructor's table and saw that he was older than he looked from across the hall. His ponytail was so tight that it stretched out his wrinkles giving him an extra large forehead and eyes which seemed to pop out of his stern scary facial expression.

There was also a strange smell coming from his direction, like the smell as you enter a department store's perfume department where a hundred potential customers have tried out aftershave and they have all compounded into a chemical nightmare. It was like that smell but with an added musty talcum powder smell.

"This is worse than we thought," whispered Grace to Sam, her eyes watering because of the stench coming from the gym instructor. Sam nodded miserably. "I haven't seen one kid, every one of these passengers look at least six times our age."

The gym instructor sneered at the kids and promptly turned the sneer into a cheesy smile as Mom turned in his direction.

"Weirdo alert," whispered Grace in Sam's ear just low enough for Mom and Dad not to hear.

In what seemed like an eternity later the silence was broken when Mom said excitedly, "Look kids! There's a kid's club. Why don't you go and check it out?". "At last ... something interesting," shouted Grace excitedly. Maybe a little too loud, as it caused many of the other passengers who had all been queuing patiently in the line in front of them, to turn and glare at her. One particularly grumpy looking gentleman made a loud tutt-ing sound and turned to his equally grumpy looking wife and said in a voice deliberately loud enough for everyone to hear. "They shouldn't allow children on this cruise. It ... so . lowers the tone."

Had Grace not seen the cautionary look Mom gave her, she would have had no problem replying to the gentleman, "That would be fine by me if children were not allowed on this lousy cruise". But the 'Scary Mom Look' reserved for serious occasions stopped Grace from speaking.

Dad totally ignored the comment, he knew it was not clever to make enemies with people you were going to share a boat with for a week. He tried to smile at them, as though acknowledging their grievance.

Meanwhile, the children turned eagerly in the direction Mom had pointed. Sure enough there was the table. Both kids were hoping that there would be some cool looking teenage cruise employees surrounded by lots of fun looking kids just their age. This vision was soon to be replaced by a different scene.

At the table were two middle aged men dressed up as clowns. The one on the left was a large man dressed in a large red clown suit. The suit was blowing bubbles out of a plastic flower attached to the top pocket. The bubbles popped pathetically as soon as they left the flower and splashed soapy water onto the table and down the red clown suit making it look as though the clown had been drooling on himself.

The other clown on the right was thinner and had a green suit. He had painted a much too large white smile on his face. Combined with the green suit, the smile made him look like an overgrown skinny frog. It did not help that he had ears which stuck out. Sam was sure one ear was much lower than the other, which concerned him. Sam squinted with each eye trying to see if the clown's ears really were at different levels. They were. On the table in front of the clowns were some crayons, coloring pages, and plastic blocks. This did not look hopeful.

To Grace and Sam's dismay, the two clowns saw the children as they stood in line. Both of the children's faces were frozen in a state of shock and horror. "Ahoy," the two clowns said together, "Come over fellow pirates. Let's get ready to sail the waves together." Great. Two grown up men dressed in clown suits, talking like pirates were going to be the sole source of entertainment for the next week. That was worse than both the kids had thought. They were not going anywhere near that table.

Mom had other ideas, "What fun," she said a little too eagerly, "Go on over kids. This line isn't going very fast. Go and see what is going on." Grace and Sam had other ideas... maybe running in the opposite direction was an option. "Pleeeeasse no," they begged. In response Dad gave a stern look to them both, "Come on. You two need to get into the spirit of this vacation. Mom will hold our place. I will come with you. Let's see what they have going on. How bad can it be? It's a kids club?" Dad placed a firm hand on Grace and Sam's shoulders and marched them over to the table.

"Hello Pirates," said the clown in green still in the same fake pirate voice, "I am 'Fizzy'. This is my fellow pirate, 'Busy'. You are going to have so much fun on this cruise at the *World Renowned Fizzy and Busy Club.* We shall have daily activities you can join in while your parents are on board relaxing or on land touring the wonderful sights."

Dad gave Froggy a big smile. Grace and Sam knew by the look on their Dad's face that he was genuinely thinking this might be a good idea. When Dad spoke it confirmed their thoughts, "My lovely wife and I are celebrating our 15th Anniversary. It would be great to have some time together. I am sure the kids would love to come along." Dad always referred to Mom as "My lovely wife". Mom loved that stuff.

Froggy then smiled and to the children's astonishment, let out a loud snort that sounded like a pig choking on sherbert powder. The kids and Dad took a step back. It was only when Froggy stopped snorting and made a weird swallowing sound that they realized the snort was actually not Froggy choking. It was his laugh.

As though to distract everyone from Froggy's weird laughter, the other clown, Busy, cleared his throat loudly and in an elaborate bow-like gesture bent forward to pick up a handwritten brochure with the title "*Fizzy and Busy DayCare Schedule*". But as he leant forward the plastic flower on his suit released a bubble, the plastic flower's best and largest bubble yet. Unfortunately, the gigantic bubble flew right into Sam's face and burst letting all the soapy liquid explode right into his horrified open eye.

"Arrrghh ahh arghhhhh!!!" screamed Sam, "He shot a bubble in my eye." Sam jumped up and down holding his left eye. This was a very loud spectacle that Sam was making and of course attracted a lot of attention from the people in line. Dad grimaced as the passengers turned around again and gave looks of hate and loud tutting in their direction. Grace was sure she saw the grumpy older man stamp his feet and tutt so loudly that his poor wife was showered in spittle.

It was then that Grace started to get the giggles. The shower of spit from the grumpy man and the fact that a large silly looking clown who thought he was a pirate had "shot" a bubble into her brother's eye made her think of a really bad movie.... maybe a Scooby-doo movie. "Zoiks – that clown shot me with a bubble," she mimicked. Then she proceeded to jump up and down and imitate Sam's scream, "Arrr arrr arghh." Then went back into a fit of giggles. Soon her giggle turned into a full on roar of laughter.

Meanwhile, Sam's eye felt better. Grace's laugh was always very addictive to him. It wasn't long before he started to laugh as well, just as loudly as Grace. Now both of them were laughing hysterically. There were even more looks of horror from the waiting passengers.

"Calm down!" hissed Dad sternly under his breath. He then turned, shrugged and smiled in embarrassment at the staring passengers and apologized profusely to the two strange clowns. He was careful to avoid Mom's glare.

It was only when Dad raised his voice, almost yelling, "Be Quiet....NOW!" that the children muffled their roaring laughter to a quiet chuckle and occasional hiccup from Grace who was trying hard, very hard, not to laugh.

Froggy, the green clown with the painted smile, was not as amused. Even Busy's smile was more of a straight line now. But he still was playing his role, "We are going to have soooo much fun fellow Pirates."

Grace thought to herself, "Please. This really cannot get any worse."

But could it? Read on to find out.

Chapter 3

Room to Roam

Finally, after what seemed like days, not hours, the family boarded the huge ship and following a map given to them at the gate, they worked their way around the labyrinth of narrow corridors, twisting and contorting themselves to get around the other passengers until they finally found their room. They were greeted by a man in the cruise line's gray uniform. He was young with dark black hair and a huge smile. He introduced himself as Joel and told us that he would be our housekeeper (or cabin keeper) for the week, then he asked the kids their names and where they were from.

His eyes twinkled as he beamed at them. The kids liked him immediately. He told Mom and Dad that if they needed anything in the cabin, they could call him as he was usually in the corridor. Mom and Dad said they would be fine for now. "Excellent," said Joel. He winked at the kids as they went in the room to unpack. They would have liked to have chatted with him longer but were equally excited to see inside their new 'home'. Remarkably their suitcases had made it to the room before them and seemed to dominate the area.

The room was so tiny.

Mom and Dad had a bed which took up most of the room at the far end of the cabin. On the left, there was a narrow door leading to an equally tiny bathroom. The children marveled at the space which was so small, yet it could contain a toilet, shower and basin. That was some amazing design. In the same room was a double bed, a bunk bed and very little space in between. In fact no room at all. Trying to find space for four people and the three suitcases was like a video game gone bad. They bumped into each other and in the end, Grace and Sam had to pile onto Mom and Dad's bed until the clothes and suitcases were crammed into a small wardrobe near the door.

"Oh, Love," said Mom, "This is great." She hugged Dad, who gleamed back at her. The children were not watching; they were arguing about who should have the top bunk. When it finally became a wrestling match on the lower bunk, Mom lost her good mood and her attention returned to the kids. "Enough," she said, "I have decided whoever is the best kid during the day gets the top bunk. Myself and Dad will decide at bedtime who that shall be."

She then began her usual list of demands before going out. "Get ready for dinner kids. Go to the bathroom. Wash your hands. Change your shirt. Sam you have to change out of shorts. The restaurant is long pants only. Grace put on your best dress. Find your shoes and put them on." Grace and Sam scrabbled to follow the long list of directions, as each fully intended to be awarded the top bunk.

On their way to the restaurant, they all felt a jolt as the ship started to sail. The 'Brilldom Cruise' was underway. Strangely, although neither Grace nor Sam would admit it, they both felt a tingle of excitement. As they walked back down the narrow corridor, rocking gently to the motion of the boat with the background sound of Mom and Dad giggling as they were jostled together and shouting random directions from the map, they passed Joel who wished them a good dinner, beaming his large friendly smile.

The dining room was overly decorated. The tables had candles, fancy napkins and a lot of silver sparkling cutlery. The tablecloths were purple and there was a sprinkle of confetti on each gold placemat. As they were shown to their seats, which were near the window, they were told this would be the table they would be at each evening, Grace and Sam glanced up at the elaborate chandeliers hanging above. Their waiter introduced himself as Reynaldo.

Reynaldo was smartly dressed in a white waiter's uniform, just like Joel's uniform but with a blindingly bleach white collar. He looked very professional yet friendly. He smiled at the kids, once again they had found someone they liked. When the kids devoured their first plate of pastas, Reynaldo delivered them extra pasta, followed by a huge multi-scoop, multi-colored ice cream. Though he paid great attention to Mom and Dad, pointing out the sights which they floated by outside, and made sure their glasses were full and meals perfect, he paid most attention to Grace and Sam.

At the end of the meal, he made Grace a pink rose out of pink folded napkins and he made Sam a blue napkin helicopter. They were both thrilled. "See you tomorrow," smiled Reynaldo as they left.

On their way back to the cabin, Sam zoomed his helicopter along the banister and Grace twiddled her rose into her hair. Everything seemed just fine until Dad said, "So kids, tomorrow Mom and I would like to go on the tour of the vineyard in the next port ... It is for adults only. Seeing as you both got on so well with Fizzy and Busy, I have booked you into their program for the day."

This was not what the kids wanted to hear, but their parents were not to be persuaded otherwise. Grace protested, "No way Dad. Those guys are so stupid." Sam held his mouth tightly shut. Of course, Sam got the top bunk that night.

Chapter 4

The Fizzy and Busy Club

The next morning started well. Joel the smiley room service guy was waiting with his cleaning supplies outside their door. He greeted them warmly and with his trademark huge smile and told them he was "Excellent". They made their way to the breakfast buffet. The breakfast buffet was a frenzy of, as Grace and Sam noted, 'old people' rushing around finding seats, piling rations of toast on their plates and balancing cups of coffee and tea.

Grace found Reynaldo, the waiter from their evening meal at the pancake making station. "Good Morning" he said smiling, "How did you sleep?" "Excellent" said Grace in her best Joel impression and giggled. Reynaldo smiled again and piled up a huge pile of yummy pancakes on her plate. Each covered in maple syrup and bacon. There were so many, that even Grace, who could eat more than anyone in the family, was officially full, maybe even over full, when she had finished.

Sam was so thrilled that they had endless hot chocolate and had four cups with whipped cream. He then found a chocolate spread that he could spread on chocolate muffins and sprinkle with chocolate chips. Sam was extra pleased with himself when he noticed Mom and Dad were so busy looking out at the view that they didn't even check his healthy eating choices. Maybe this cruise thing wasn't so bad he thought as he stuffed the last of the muffin into his mouth.

But, then he remembered what the day had ahead of them entailed; a day filled with the 'World Renowned Fizzy and Busy Kids Club' and that is where the feeling of contentment screeched to a stop.

Back they went down the corridor. They passed Joel who was busy tidying the cabin next door. "Anything fun planned today kids?" Joel called them. "Mom and Dad are off on the vineyard tour." explained Sam. "Excellent." said Joel, smiling. "And we are off to the Fizzy and Busy club," said Grace miserably. "Not excellent." said Joel sympathetically, his smile fading with compassion.

"What do you do during the day Joel ?" asked Sam.

"We get a few hours of free time after the cabins are finished." Joel replied, smiling again. "Normally, we catch up on sleep but today my friend Reynaldo and I are going on shore. I think Naldo is your waiter. He told me he had some cool kids on his shift. You are easy to spot since there aren't too many kids your age on this cruise line. Usually they go on the Ponder cruise. Much more fun for kids I think."

Grace looked around for her parents as though to justify her Power Point presentation. But they had already made their way inside their cabin next door. Not fair.

Before they had time to chat with Joel, Mom stuck her head out of the door and into the hall. "Come on kids. Time to get ready." Joel shared another sympathetic look with the kids. "Good luck you two. See you later."

Inside the cabin, Mom hustled and bustled to get them both to brush teeth and for Sam to wipe the chocolate off his face. Then it was back past Joel and up to the third floor where the 'Fizzy and Busy Kid's Club' was located. This time they had no illusions. It was going to be bad.

Busy was there to greet them. His red clown suit had been replaced by another suit. Today, Busy was in a suit which could only be described as a cross between a gnome suit and a banana. It was a bright yellow suit with a yellow pointy hat. The suit had brown buttons down the front which stretched so tightly over his belly. So tightly that Sam flinched in case one shot out into his eye. He wanted no more eye incidents after the bubble attack yesterday. Luckily the thread held ... at least for now.

The threat that the button may break at any minute made Sam more than a little nervous, especially as the widest spot and therefore the tightest spot on Busy's large belly was right at Sam's eye-level. Sam dodged from one foot to the other making sure he stood out of the potential line of fire. Getting bored of this, he averted his gaze and looked down at Busy's feet.

Busy had on brown boots, which looked either like the boots of a badly dressed gnome or maybe it was supposed to be the stem of the banana. As he was dressed solely in yellow the banana stem theory would have been certain evidence that he was dressed as a banana not as a gnome. But being logically minded Sam decided if he was really trying to be a banana the stem should be at the top. Right? The hat definitely looked on the gnomeish side.

Taking his banana theory a step further, Sam decided he could not imagine the rather overweight Busy standing on his head for long and even if he could manage to, Sam was sure his buttons would burst. No kid would want to be around to see that.

Sam concluded Busy was supposed to be a gnome, a very yellow gnome ... with large, very brown feet.

As Mom and Dad continued to answer Busy's lengthy questions about telephone numbers and cabin numbers, food allergies and medical questions, Grace and Sam discussed Busy's peculiar choice of clothes. Grace, who was a bit fed up with the whole situation, simply concluded Busy was a Banana Gnome and looked totally ridiculous. Whatever he was, the children were sure of two things: one Busy the Banana Gnome had big feet ... really big feet and secondly, it was a really, really bad costume.

Behind him on the carpet was Fizzy or Froggy as the kids had renamed him. Froggy had on a very lame superhero costume. He must really like green as his costume was green, just like the day before but this time a tight green suit with a green cape and to round it all off white boots and a white eye mask. Sam, once again, had the vision of a huge skinny frog with a large fat long tongue which flicked out in slow motion to swipe a passing fly. Disgusted, he shook this vision away.

At last the paperwork was done, and Busy turned to them … "Ahoy there. Welcome Pirates" said Busy. "Oh my," muttered Grace to Sam, "Now he is a Banana gnome talking Pirate. What is next, a Giraffe-Pirate talking tomato?" Sam laughed. His sister had a certain way with words.

"How are yee all doing on this mighty fine morning shipmates?" said the banana-gnome-pirate.

There was a lengthy silence. The children's faces froze in disbelief that this was really happening and furthermore that they had to spend the whole day with this man and his sidekick.

Mom nudged Grace hard, gave her a glare and Grace mumbled… "Good…em..goodish…. I guess." She thought hard about acquiring the top bunk tonight and forced a smile. Mom smiled back at her encouragingly, then turned her attention to Sam, who whimpered audibly. But, Sam also had his eye on having the top bunk bed again tonight and had decided to stay on Mom and Dad's good side. He dug deep, grimaced a smile and tried to convince himself this was worth it. He took a deep breath and proceeded to attempt to speak 'pirate' and he started out well. "I am mighty fine, fellow sailor," he said to the banana-gnome-pirate. Mom smiled, thinking Sam was really getting into the spirit of things. Grace made a face at him, knowing she was losing ground on the prestigious top bunk.

In Sam's head, he had seen Mom's approving look and was busily measuring the points he was accumulating towards having the top bunk tonight. Encouraged by the effectiveness of his pirate talk, he continued.

But, for some reason he switched from a pure pirate accent to a pirate in Yoda talk. Mixing words up like Yoda but maintaining a pirate accent "Today what here be yee doing?" He should have stopped there but he didn't.

He continued and meant to say "Never mind, to me it looks like crazy fun" but in pirate Yoda it came out "To me mind, it looks like never fun. Crazy."

Grace cracked up laughing. She laughed doubly hard when she saw Mom glaring at Sam. Sam, seeing the error of his ways but the humor, could not help but laugh too, even though he could rapidly see his bonus top bunk points fading away into the distance. But there was no doubt it was funny. Cool Jedi-master Yoda was speaking pirate and telling a fat banana gnome pirate that he was 'crazy' and that his club was stupid. It simply was funny. Don't you think?

Mom, still glaring at them both, gave one final warning eye raise to them and left hand in hand with Dad. They were alone.

Chapter 5

The Storeroom

The kids immediately stopped laughing. This was serious. They really had to stay here. They were each given a tight white bracelet with their names and cabin number written on. Now they felt like prison inmates.

Sam had contemplated running after them, screaming "Don't leave us!!" grabbing the sleeve of Mom's blouse and refusing to let go. But deciding this would be totally uncool, would not help on the top bunk point chart and, more to the point, was very unlikely to change his parent's mind about leaving them, he turned and very reluctantly followed behind Grace who had already concluded protests were pointless. They miserably followed Busy's oversized brown boots into the depths of the 'Fizzy and Busy Kid's Club'.

They soon discovered there was not actually much to explore.

On the carpet, sat in a circle headed by Superhero Froggy costumed in that green outfit, were six very somber looking children. Their ages probably ranged from between 2 to 3 years and judging by the smell, at least one of them was still in diapers, if not all of them. The somber six were looking at Froggy open mouthed as though he was speaking a different language, and maybe he was.

Froggy was sitting with his skinny legs crossed on the blue flowered carpet, his green cape flowing out behind him. Again Sam had his vision, it was certainly not difficult to imagine Froggy being a very thin frog sitting on a lily pad (the flowered carpet) and that the children were flies, unaware of their fate.

Sam shook his head once again. He really had to stop imagining this stuff. In reality, Froggy was leading the unfortunate children in a hand clapping game, which was not going well. One child who could stand it no longer had her bottom lip trembling, burst into tears. Another boy crawled away to the furthest corner and sat quite contentedly under a table rotating his activities from noisily sucking his thumb to picking his nose.

On top of the table behind them was an orange plastic tablecloth which had definitely seen better days, some coloring paper and broken crayons.

Grace and Sam scanned the rest of the area. Other than a cupboard of beaten up puzzles and games, there was nothing else notable. The two turned away from the circle of toddler madness and into a smaller alcove to the right of the 'Lilipad'.

In this area there was another carpet, this time with seashells on it and a television. Sam and Grace looked hopefully at the screen, maybe this was what they could do all day. But no such luck, as watching mesmerized were two twin boys of maybe 3 or 4 years old. They were watching 'Sesame Street.' The screen showed Elmo, who was introducing the letter "Y".

Sam groaned. "Y(why) - I ask you?". " Y (why) us," replied Grace, feeling his pain. They looked around for a remote control so maybe they could persuade the twins another channel would be more fun. The television was too high to reach and remote was their only hope. They scanned the area.

On the left were the restrooms and in the far corner opposite the television was another door marked 'Private'. Maybe this is where they kept the remote. There must be one. Grace and Sam could not imagine Busy stretching up to the television without popping at least one of his buttons and Froggy looked way too small to reach. It had to be somewhere lower down. The door marked 'Private' was the only hope.

The children quickly looked back around the corner towards the entrance. Busy, the banana gnome pirate, was 'busy' doing nothing at the front gate, doodling on the clipboard and staring out into the hallway. Maybe he should be renamed 'Lazy,' thought Grace.

'Super Hero' Froggy, was busy trying to quiet a now screaming toddler while entertaining the others. He picked up some juggling balls and for a moment the child stopped screaming. That was until Froggy tripped on his cape and one of the balls landed on the same child's head. That kid was not having a good day. The other kids seemed to think it was getting a little more entertaining though and even the kid under the table came out to see if there was any more action.

Taking advantage of this diversion, Grace poked Sam to get his attention and motioned towards the door marked 'Private'. It did not take more than a millisecond for Sam to be convinced they should investigate what was in there. "*Even if there was not a television remote,*" he thought, "*Maybe they could hide there for a while away from the madness.*"

Grace was surprised to find that when she turned the handle it was unlocked. Her practical mind thought it was a safety issue to have a door to a private area unlocked. Even if all the kids were super respectful of rules, more than half of them were too young to read. She pushed open the unlocked door, which creaked to reveal a rather musty and very dark room. There was another creak as the door swung closed behind them, followed by a panicked whisper from Grace, "I can't see". Then there was a bang and a louder more urgent cry from Grace, "Oww".

Sam did not hesitate; he reached into his pocket and took out the Magigad 3000: the gadget which he had begged Mom and Dad to buy him for his Birthday. As the adverts claimed, "the Magigad 3000 is a key ring sized gadget full of multiple tools and accessories no child or adult can do without". Even Grace at that moment, who often rolled her eyes when Sam went into a speech about the awesomeness of the Magigad, would have to agree, right now it did have its uses. Sam pressed a button and a strong flashlight shone around the room, illuminating dusty shelves and old stationary. It looked like a storage room.

It seemed large in comparison to the play area and was full of junk; some interesting looking junk, an old computer, papers, books and then other less interesting junk; more tubs of broken crayons, baby toys and half opened snack bags. Everything was covered in dust. The half empty snack bags seemed to explain the unappetizing, musty smell. Sam shone the Magigad back to the door and found what he thought was the lightswitch. He switched it on. A lone light bulb on a wire swung above him, casting a faint but sure light across the room. A spider's web swung in rhythm with the lamp. Sam, who was more than a little scared of spiders looked around for the spider, momentarily distracted from Grace's cry.

Flashing the Magigad light further into the room over the various grades of junk, he saw Grace lying feet in the air and with her head under the lower shelf. "*That explained the bang and Oww*," thought Sam. "Are you OK?" he questioned, climbing over to his sister.

"Yes," said Grace calmly, "I am just fine. I fell over something and ..." With her head still under the shelf, she artfully twisted her body around into a crawling position so that her feet were no longer sticking in an unladylike manner in the air. Instead of her feet, now it was her bottom that stuck up in the air. "I'm sort of stuck here ..." she continued.

Sam waited a moment. Long enough to realize it was true, she was not coming out from under the shelf anytime soon. He knelt down next to her and asked again "Are you sure you are fine Grace?" "Yes I am fine," repeated Grace calmly. There was another pause and some creaking noises. Grace's head stayed under the shelf, her bottom wiggled and there were some straining noises as though she was lifting something heavy. "Grace ..." said Sam slowly wondering if his sister had maybe banged her head on the shelf and lost her mind. "Mmmm yes," replied Grace, her voice muffled by the shelf. "Are you coming out?" asked Sam. Grace backed up and turned to face her brother.

"Sam. You would never guess what is under the shelf." she whispered with a strange look of excitement in her eyes. "Dust?" said Sam, concluding she had probably banged her head. He began to envision himself having to carry her out and deliver the news of her 'madness' to a superhero and a banana gnome and eight children under the age of four.

"*Hmm*" he thought "*Maybe that wouldn't be too bad. Maybe they would have to contact Mom and Dad back from their tour and he could get out of here? Living with a crazy sister could not be that much harder than living with her now...? If it would get him out of this place ...*"

Grace began talking excitedly. "Sam, there is a trapdoor under the shelf. It slides open and leads to some stairs. If we crawl under the shelf backwards we can get to it and lower ourselves down the stairs. Let's see where it goes," she pleaded. Sam considered the facts: Grace could be hallucinating, concussed or telling the truth. If she was in fact not delusional, but telling the truth, the stairs could be a much better alternative than returning back into 'Diaperville'. Maybe they could escape. Either way, he had to find out.

Chapter 6

The Escape

"Let me see," said Sam eagerly, almost pushing Grace aside. Here was his chance to see if she had in fact gone completely mad.

He got on all fours, stuck his butt in the air and maneuvered his head carefully under the shelf into the spot that Grace had just retreated from. He shone the Magigad on the floor. He was lucky, as he nearly dropped the Magigad down the hole which was right in front of him. Grace was not hallucinating. She had fallen and knocked what looked like a sliding trap door open. Sam could see with his light that the opening Grace had revealed led to metal stairs. He balanced himself more securely, so he would not fall, and shone the light down further. He could see about ten stairs leading onto concrete. He squinted and wiggled the Magigad into different angles but could see no further.

Sam backed up fast, banging his head in his excitement. "Let's go," he exclaimed, rubbing his head. "It is an escape made just for us." Grace had the same glimmer of excitement in her eyes but, during the few minutes that Sam had been under the shelf, she had been worrying that if they explored further, they would be discovered.

"Let's go back and see what they are doing. If they are not looking for us we will sneak back here. We don't want them to send out a search party. They may think we have been lost overboard," Grace reasoned semilogically.

"Don't be silly," replied Sam for once, not feeling logical at all. Usually, he was the practical one but this time he felt over powered by the need for adventure. "*Maybe it was the sea*," he thought. Pondering himself on his unusual lack of reason. He had to convince Grace to come.

"Those idiots couldn't remember how many socks they put on this morning, let alone how many kids they have been left in charge of. Let's just go." Sam pleaded.

He was worried if they entered back into the Fizzy and Busy Club, they would never be able to return and that was not the way he wanted his day to go. He was not scared of getting into trouble. He was pretty sure that after calling an adult crazy earlier during his Yoda Pirate speech, it had already lost him the chance of the top bunk anyway (even if that adult had been wearing the worst costume made for man and most people would agree with him that Busy was in fact crazy). Mom was a stickler for politeness. There was absolutely no way she would forget. Plus he could almost smell adventure and was ready to go.

But Grace was already by the door. "I'm just going to check," she said, then cautiously opened the door and snuck off in the direction of the carpet of gloom. "Why does she have to choose now to be the sensible one?" grumbled Sam to himself. He decided not to protest.

Resigned, he sat down on the floor, under the swinging lightbulb, switched his Magigad into gaming mode, pulled out the retractable headphones from the cleverly concealed plug compartment and played a game while he waited. He was not going back into the smelly diaper world if he could help it. "*Man the Magigad is cool*" he thought and settled down to concentrate on the game.

Grace crept quietly past the television. Elmo had finished, and it was now blaring out some other 'below 3 year old favorite' which Grace did not recognize. The twins however were no longer watching. The other room was quiet too and as she turned the corner she could see the whole club was empty. At the front door Busy was sitting with his feet up on the desk, earphones in his ears snoring loudly. Maybe they were all out hunting for them ... "*Oh no, we are going to be in so much trouble.*" she thought sadly to herself. With a big sigh she walked closer to Busy, meaning to hand herself in and stop the search party.

As she got closer she realized she was going to have a job waking Busy up. He looked very comfortable and through the loud snores she could hear Disney tunes blaring through his headphones from his Ipod. Then she saw the sign on the counter "Gone on Pirate Boat tour back after lunch". Had they all left without them? Without noticing ? This was too good to be true.

In front of Busy on his desk lay the clipboard where Busy had signed them in earlier. Grace scanned it making sure there were no notes about escapees. In fact there were no notes at all.

Grace feared for the safety of all those under five year olds in Busy and Froggy's care but was also super relieved that due to their incompetence, the ship was not being searched for them. Feeling very brave she went one step further and picked up the pen. Nervously she marked a cross by their names under the column marked 'released'. After pausing briefly to ponder why they had used the word 'released', instead of 'checked out' or some word less prison-like, just a momentary thought as she joyfully rushed back towards the storeroom. She was convinced that even if Froggy or Busy remembered they existed they would check the clipboard and think they had been returned to their parents, or rather, 'released' back to their parents. Genius. She sped back to Sam.

"Get up. Get up," she shouted excitedly. "We are free. We are free. We can go." Even with his headphones on, he could hear her. He jumped up immediately, hurriedly put the Magigad safely into his pocket and called, "Me first. Me first." Before Grace could argue, he had turned around and was sliding into the space under the shelf, feet first so he could bend himself down into the stairway below. As Grace followed and they both shuffled down the stairs, Grace filled Sam in on what had happened at the front desk. She carefully closed the trapdoor above them, as a precaution. But in reality if anyone followed the trail of dust they had left behind in the storeroom, they would certainly be found out.

On hearing Grace's story Sam confirmed Grace's opinion. "Genius Grace," he stated clearly impressed, then he added, "I didn't know you had it in you."

Grace decided to ignore Sam's last remark and climbed downwards after her brother's disappearing shadow. When both of their feet were on the concrete ground, Sam shone the bright light of the Magigad 3000 around them.

Chapter 7

Chutes and Slides

The room was very small. The only things of note were some shelves with towels and linens on and a white closed door with a peep hole. It smelt very strongly of laundry detergent.

As they looked behind them, it was difficult to find the stairs from which they had entered the room. A strange swing door had concealed the stairs' whereabouts, fitting so flush to the wall that had they not just entered the room this way, they would not have spotted anything there. *"Funny"* thought Sam, *"I don't remember pushing a door open."*

He turned back around and focused the Magigad light on the door and in particular at the peephole. "I call dibs on first look," said Grace quickly getting her own back for coming down the stairs last.

As she pressed her eye tight onto the peephole Grace could see what looked like a laundry room with lots of washers and dryers. They were the huge front loading machines like the ones you might expect in a launderette. The dull buzz of dryers could be heard through the wall and a strong smell of starch and bleached added to the already pungent smell of laundry detergent.

"It's just a laundry room," reported Grace, a little disappointed. She had expected something more than this, maybe they had just found an old laundry chute. *"How boring,"* she thought. But at least they had escaped 'The World Renowned Fizzy and Busy Club'. Maybe they could just explore the ship for a while. But they would risk the chance of bumping into the Frog and the rest of the Diaper Club? Hmm no chance. That would be bad. Maybe the door didn't open anyway.

She looked back through the hole at the laundry room to see where the exit door was located. It was then that she heard that very door open followed by footsteps coming, and there were voices. "All clear," said one voice. "Excellent" replied another voice. This voice was vaguely familiar "Opening the GMSC."

A loud click and buzzing sound began.

Sam could sense Grace's agitation. "What's going on?" he asked. "Shhhh," replied Grace in a growling whisper, "Stay quiet. There is someone there."

One of the huge washing machines opposite the peephole had popped open. Instead of the usual big silver tumbler inside there was a chute. This silver glittery chute was lit up part of the way but led into complete darkness which seemed to imply that it went a long way.

"There is a chute inside a washing machine straight in front of this door." Grace reported back to Sam in a quiet whisper. "I wonder where it goes? And why? Is it another laundry chute?" She added as though talking to herself.

Being a great problem solver (not to mention that he felt a little left out not being able to see), Sam switched his Magigad into Navigation Mode and knelt down. Pointing the screen between Grace's legs and aligning the arrows on his screen. It took a second for the report to come up on the screen but when it did, Sam could see that the chute apparently led straight through the walls of the boat, across a small stretch of water and onto land.

"According to the Magigad Navigation Mode, it seems to go through the wall and across onto land," reported Sam to Grace.

"Oh wow, a secret exit to the port." murmured Grace still in a whisper, "It is definitely a secret tunnel. I thought there was supposed to be only one entrance and exit. Remember that weird cruise staff guy who checked our documents. He told us the only exit was that one way or on a lifeboat or a coffin! He was so not funny. Even Mom didn't laugh and she laughed at everything. He did that weird cackling laugh you see on vampire cartoons. I didn't think people actually did that."

She paused, remembering the scene then focused back on the matter at hand, reporting back up to her brother. "The opening to the chute seems more like the start of a tube slide you might find at a playground rather than an exit or maybe as it crosses the sea, like an entrance to a waterpark."

"Maybe it's where they bring on and off supplies." answered Sam practically. Once again he resumed the role of the voice of logic.

"Through a washing machine, Sam? I don't think so." Grace replied. She was sure this was something more exciting than a mere trade entrance.

"Oh I forgot it was inside a washing machine." Sam said a little sarcastically, shutting down the Magigad Navigation mode. "Remember I cannot see, as you are hogging the view. Budge over and let me see." He moved closer, pushing Grace slightly, in an attempt to get a better view.

Grace could hear the voices approaching the peephole. Sam heard voices too and strained to look into the small peephole with his sister. Grace gently, but firmly, pushed him aside. "Shhhh," she repeated. Sam resigned his position at the peephole and laid down looking through the crack under the door. He watched as two sets of shoes walked by. Sam was so low down he could only see their shoes; one pair of very clean sneakers and one highly polished set of black shoes stopped parallel to the door. Grace of course got a full face view but even Sam could tell who at least one of the voices belonged to, by their conversation.

"Are you ready?" The first voice said, "Cannot wait to meet up and go to the Lodge, maybe we will have time to go to the Volcanite Zone. What do you think?" "Excellent," said the second voice, "Let's slide." The mere word 'excellent' from the second voice was the giveaway. "It's Joel," hissed Sam "... and Reynaldo," exclaimed Grace quietly. She still had a much better viewpoint, "They are going down the tube." The sneakers and shiny shoes moved away and there was a whoosh noise as Joel and Reynaldo exited down the chute.

Grace did not hesitate. "Let's follow them," she muttered and turned the handle of the door, relieved to find it opened easily. "Quick in case the washing machine door closes." Sam was just glad the door opened outwards, otherwise it would have hit him hard in the face, as he was still laid looking under the crack at the bottom of the door. Relieved, Sam jumped up and rushed across the passageway in hot pursuit of Grace. They jumped in the huge washing machine, just in time, before the round glass door locked with a click behind them.

Chapter 8

Magical Folk and Acronyms

Inside was very dark and super fast. Grace was right, the chute seemed to go on much longer than she could imagine when she looked through the peephole.

As it twisted left and right, the children gathered up more speed as it got much steeper. Grace felt excitement and a little bit of alarm as they were jolted back and forth towards a round light which got closer and closer. They could see the end. Grace closed her eyes tight, unsure of how they would land at this speed but she need not worry. There was a final 'whoosh' sound before they piled out, one after the other, onto a soft bed of what seemed to be moss. "Woah," spluttered Sam who followed close behind, "That was cool." He found himself submerged up to his waist in bright green moss. He brushed the moss off his face and looked around.

"Where did the others go?" Sam questioned, looking around for Joel and Reynaldo unsure of what they would think of the kid invasion. With all the moss around him he had expected to be outside, but instead they were in another small room with no windows. The Magigad Navigation had not predicted a room. Moss was everywhere. Even on the walls. It lay in various sized mounds across the floor. The children had landed on a pile which was by far the largest and messiest. The other piles seemed more organized and almost groomed. Surrounding the piles, near the edge of the room there was a curious circular area on the floor clear from the moss which touched every other area the children could see. The circle glistened like silver and shone like a mirror. If you looked closer it had an intricate pattern on it like when frost interweaves a pattern onto a windowpane in winter and twinkles in the morning sunshine. The circle radiated all the light in the room.

Sam wanted to touch the circle, but he hesitated, afraid to get off the moss and onto the twinkling floor, in case it really was glass and broke beneath him. Grace equally surprised by their strange port of arrival and curious about the radiating circle of light stuttered, "Wwwhere on earth are we?" She bravely shuffled carefully towards the end of the bed of moss and dangled her legs over the edge of the circle of light.

"It is not exactly Earth," answered a voice

"And don't jump off the moss just yet," agreed another voice.

Two heads simultaneously popped up out of the mound of unkempt moss. Joel and Reynaldo shook the moss out of their hair and smiled at the kids. "Phew," exclaimed Reynaldo, obviously relieved. "We were hiding, we thought you were 'the Weavers'. Hi Grace, Hi Sam. How ever did you manage to find the slide?"

Joel, still pulling the moss out of his hair, laughed at the kid's explanation. "Excellent job kids. You escaped the Fizzy and Busy Club. Staged a breakout. Congratulations. I know Fizzy and Busy are not the most observant but no one has ever escaped. Good job. Oh and we certainly did not expect anyone to be following us down the GMSC. Scared us to bits. I was hiding in the moss so long

I think I ate enough greens to last a week." He picked a bit of moss out of his teeth. "Man," he exclaimed to Reynaldo, "I really thought the Weavers had followed us."

"Any way to get you to eat more vegetables buddy." joked Reynaldo. "You are worse than the oldies on the ship. Some of them hide the sprouts under their forks; as though I would tell them off."

Grace was less interested in old people's eating habits and more interested in where they were and what was going on. "The GMSC? " she asked, confused, "What is that ?"

"Oh the GMSC is the Glass Moss Slide Chute fondly known as the Glosser," explained Reynaldo, "The port of entry to the MFL."

"I have heard of the NFL," commented Sam, "but what is the MFL?"

"Do you always talk in acronyms ?" Grace asked, a little frustrated. "It is very confusing."

"MFL is the Magical Folk Local, affectionately known as the Muffle. In this port, the Muffle is called the Enchanted Lodge. Most ports have a Muffle." Reynaldo explained patiently, "Each port has a secret entrance to the Muffle for that city. It is usually under the earth's crust. More precisely in the narrow layers between the lithosphere and asthenosphere. Magical folk meet there to stay if they are visiting, but also to trade things at the local Demi Market or to head to the Volconite Zone for a PAA or a Potentially Amazing Adventure if you are not talking in acronyms. They can also get their Trackle." He paused to think. "Funny ....Trackle doesn't have an acronym " he observed "Maybe it is an acronym T.R.A.C.K.L.E ? I wonder."

"What is an acronym again?" asked Sam. Before Reynaldo could answer Grace sighed and gave Reynaldo and Joel a slightly embarrassed glance. "Look it up on your Magigad dictionary app" she hissed. "You are embarrassing yourself dude."

Taking his sister at her word, Sam read aloud from his Magigad dictionary app fully aware this would embarrass Grace further... "An acronym is an abbreviation formed from the initial components in a phrase or a word. Usually these components are individual letters (as in NATO or USA) or parts of words or names. (As in Benelux, which is an acronym for Belgium, the Netherlands and Luxembourg). Cool."

Grace rolled her eyes but silently had to admit to herself that she did not know the Benelux was an acronym.

"Cool gadget," Joel interrupted, edging closer to Sam by wading through the moss "You have a Magigad? Which version? Can I see? I always wanted one of those."

Sam was about to share his cool facts about the Magigad 3000 when Reynaldo shouted "Look out." The trapdoor above their heads opened and an object shot out just missing Grace's head and became submerged into the moss.

Grace leapt away from the projectile object and half swam, half crawled across the moss towards Joel, Reynaldo and Sam, who had at lightning speed moved to the other side of the moss mound. Their heads submerged under the green moss. Grace froze, then followed suit, plunging her head into the moss.

The trapdoor slid closed above their heads and there was an eerie silence.

Chapter 9

Pixel arrives.

Grace was debating what to do next. The moss was soft and light but Joel was right, it got everywhere. You could not fail but swallow some and it tasted like the smell of seaweed and cabbage. She was also sure it was sticking to her hair. Fortunately, she didn't have to wait long until the moss quivered, Joel and Reynaldo stuck their heads out and gave the all clear.

Trustfully, Grace rose up, picked the moss out of her eyelashes and waited until her vision cleared to reveal who or what had been the missile. She carefully scanned across the green. Grace's eyes met with Sam who was looking equally confused. Then she saw two tiny hands sticking out from the moss, not far from Sam. Pretty pink nail polish and a sparkly twinkling bracelet were clearly visible, contrasting dramatically with the green of the surrounding moss. Next came two arms and a head of golden blonde hair delicately braided into neat braids, tied with sparkly and twinkly bands matching the bracelet. A pretty yet impish looking face followed. It would have been extremely pretty apart from the expression on her face. Her eyes were pinched together and her nose slightly squinted.

"Achoo," she sneezed loudly into her elbow. "Drat this lousy moss," she complained "Why does he think it is a good thing to land in this toxic mess? Lemon Balm seeds would be much better, they are soft yet not so ... mossy"

"Well Hello Pixel," called Reynaldo, "So glad you and your good attitude could come."

Pixel's face transformed as she grinned broadly. She was in fact very pretty. She clearly had not noticed Grace or Sam yet. "Naldo, Joel how are you? Check this out."

She proceeded to fiddle with her bracelet and suddenly two wings shot out from a small backpack she was wearing. She laughed and flung herself into the air. She proceeded to flutter around, mostly somersaulting. It was impressive but maybe a little uncoordinated. She finished in a grand finale which could only be described as various versions of aerial jolty star jumps. She looked like a first grader who was extremely happy to be taking trampoline lessons for the first time, except Pixel was so much smaller. Pixel was tiny. Her aerial display was not the most graceful thing Grace had ever seen and certainly not how Grace had ever imagined she would behave if she suddenly sprouted wings. Grace imagined herself gliding around like a superhero but instead of a cape, she had Pixel's beautiful wings. As Pixel entered into the jolty star part of her display Grace suddenly became conscious that her mouth was open in astonishment, awe, confusion? She was not quite sure which one. What was she looking at? Was she looking at a fairy? No way fairies do not exist.

Pixel was also not dressed as Grace imagined a fairy would be dressed. That was if Grace still believed in fairies and if she believed Pixel was in fact a real fairy. Pixel had on a silver T-shirt with the name Pixel written on it in fancy bright pink writing. Her silver wings poked through the back and looked as though they had been there all the time, even though they had just witnessed her shooting them out of her back. If she wasn't a real fairy, she had done a great job with the wings. They had a sheen like a dragonfly's wing which had been covered in glitter glue.

She had denim jeans on with pockets covered in tiny green sequins which shimmered like the feathers of a kingfisher. She was indeed very trendy and reminded Grace of a tiny celebrity YouTuber.

Sam was not so much grading the display or critiquing her fashion, but he was trying to figure Pixel out. Was she some kind of girl genius who had invented a backpack with mechanical wings? That would be so cool. Sam loved gadgets, he immediately wanted to know how it worked. But she was so small. Much tinier and daintier than a regular girl. What was he seeing? A hologram? A cyborg? A fairy? No way fairies did not exist. Joel and Reynaldo must be playing tricks on them with some kind of hologram.

The hologram floated down gently and landed next to Sam. "What did you think?" she asked him, trying to curtsey but stumbling in the moss and coughing loudly.

"Cool," spluttered Sam who also had been covered in moss when she landed. He couldn't resist it. He reached out and touched her arm. On finding that it was in fact a real arm, he did an embarrassing fake fall as though he had stumbled and touched her by accident. He must have been convincing because she instinctively grabbed his arm to help him balance. Pixel was definitely not a hologram.

"Woah dude." She said to Sam as they both fell backwards into the moss.

"Well Pixel," Naldo announced "You have met one of our new friends, allow me to introduce you officially to Grace and Sam. They are fugitives on the run from the Fizzy and Busy club. We are very proud to say they are the only ones ever to escape with their life and sanity."

Grace giggled at the idea of being fugitives. Naldo continued, "This is Grace. Hair bigger than the state of Texas, more beautiful than the flowers of Hawaii, wilder than the trails of the Blue Ridge mountains of Virginia and the color of the forests in Fall in Vermont. Yet I do not believe that her head just has hair, I do not doubt that she has a brain just as big and awesome."

Sam agreed and if in fact 'Grace's Hair' was a state in the USA, her hair would be the state of Texas. Her hair had always been big, bold, amber- blond and totally untamable. Her hair was always commented on wherever they went. You certainly did not want to sit behind her at the movies. You would not be able to see. Plus, Naldo was right, she was pretty smart, if her grades at school were anything to go by. That Naldo was pretty astute.

Reynaldo (Naldo) turned his attention to Sam. 'Now Pixel, this is Sam or Samuel. To describe him in US landmarks; he has a smile as wide as the Mississippi River is long, heart as deep as Niagara falls, he is brighter than Time Square on New Year's Eve and he is aspiring to have more electronics in his life than in Silicon Valley."

It was Pixel's turn to beam. She bounced up and down on the moss, clapping her hands. "Do me!! Do me!!" She shouted excitedly, eager to hear Naldo describe her.

"Okay." mused Naldo as he rubbed his chin and looked quizzically at her 'Hmm!"

"Do it !! Do it!!" demanded Pixel squealing impatiently.

"Samuel, Grace, " Naldo said theatrically, "May I introduce Pixel, our very good friend and fairy travel companion. She is louder than New Orleans during Mardi Gras, crazier than Los Angeles in rush hour and more annoying than the mosquitoes of the Great Lakes in summertime." He finished his assessment with a huge laughing fit.

Pixel meanwhile faked her disappointment. "Oh Joel. Naldo is being mean. Tell Grace and Sam that, that description isn't true".

"Pretty accurate. I'd say," laughed Joel "Oh other than I would describe you more as a 'travel Pixie' than a 'travel Fairy'. Your ears are much larger than a regular fairy's ears."

"You are right Joel" teased Naldo, stifling his laughter "and technically her wings are just a little more pointy."

"Ouuugh! You boys. I don't know why I keep you as friends. You are so rude," she leapt into the air, fluttering over to Naldo, turning her back and fluttering her wings so fast she looked like a hummingbird. Naldo sneezed as the moss rose into the air around him.

"Stop it," he half laughed, half sneezed.

Pixel's revenge was interrupted by a loud siren. She stopped and took a seat on the moss, which gradually floated back down and settled. "I love this bit," she squeaked excitedly, apparently having forgotten her anger. "Grace, Sam, come sit near the middle!! Quick quick! Time for the CFP. Where is Geeko?"

Grace and Sam scrambled over to where the others were sitting, wondering what CFP was and if the acronyms would ever end. They couldn't keep track. But, there wasn't time for an explanation.

Above, the trap door chute opened once again and an object rocketed down, this time narrowly missing Sam. Nobody had time to hide this time. Whatever it was dived deep into the moss. It then rose up above the green to reveal a pointy red hat followed by a chubby grinning face and big dark sunglasses. "Greetings all!" it shouted above the noise of the siren. It was what could only be described as a smiley bespectacled gnome-like creature. *"The day just got even weirder,"* thought Sam.

"You are sooooo late," chastised Pixel in an equally loud voice, "You almost missed it."

Sam and Grace barely had time to wonder what he would have missed, when the siren stopped and the moss floor rose from the silver circle surrounding them. The moss covered floor began to spin like a carousel faster and faster. The moss flew out from underneath them and onto the walls then they too were gently but firmly pushed out onto the walls of the room. "Yehaaaw!" yelled the Gnome CFL Centrifugal Porthole," here we come!!"

"*Centrifugal force*" thought Grace remembering her science class last year. "The energy caused by the spinning forced objects to the outside surface," she muttered partly to herself and partly explaining to Sam.

Grace's class had done an experiment last spring with a glass full of liquid firmly attached and spinning on a potter's wheel as fast as the kids could spin it. It had been a fun (and messy) experiment. The water had been pushed from the bottom of the bottle to the sides as the potter's wheel spun faster.

"CFP ... Centrifugal Force Porthole." Grace deciphered.

Sam was not thinking about science, he was enjoying the buzz of adrenalin. He had with a struggle managed to pull his Magigad out of his pocket. The centrifugal force made it hard to defy gravity and lift your arms. He had hit the camera option and was recording the blur as he whizzed round. "Yeahaaaaaar !" he screamed, his voice catching up to him on the way round causing him to giggle and continue shouting.

His laughing stopped when he looked down and saw that all of the moss (and himself, Grace, Naldo, Joel, Pixel and the gnome-like figure) had been forced sidewards from the floor onto the walls. The floor was now just shimmering, shiny glass like the shiny circle around moss had been. Slowly the floor started to drop from beneath them and fall, revealing a giant hole below. The floor had completely disappeared. Sam gulped and began to feel very nervous. Nevertheless, he pointed his Magigad down and recorded the empty void below.

Though the centrifugal force had made it hard to move any part of your body, Grace had also looked down nervously at the vast void beneath them and then looked around at the others. Pixel, Naldo, Joel and the Gnome-like fellow all seemed to be fully enjoying themselves, their faces slightly distorted as the centrifugal force pushed them back. Their joy slightly reassured her that it might actually be okay.

Pixel's ponytails were high above her, flattened against the wall. The gnome's hat was also squished against the wall but amazingly still stayed perched on his head. Grace wondered what her hair looked like. With effort, she moved her hand above her head and felt around. Yes her hair was flattened to the wall, circling her head like a lion's mane.

Naldo was laughing, with effort he had pushed his hand in front of him and was making waves, just like a child with his hand outside the opened window of a moving car. Up and down. Up and down. Grace was tempted to do the same but kept her hands flat against the wall. This felt safer to her, as she felt if she moved a finger away from the wall, she might just fall.

Pixel looked over at Grace and Sam, saw their nervous faces and shouted. "Follow me!!" She crunched herself into a ball, tucked in her head to her knees, somehow her wings had vanished. She tucked up tight and cannon-balled right into the middle of the room, where she was swiftly sucked down into the giant hole below.

"Cannonball !!" shouted Joel and did the same. Knees tucked into his chin, eyes closed, he too plunged into the hole with all the joy of a child on a hot day about to splash into a cool pool."

"Don't be scared. Follow us" shouted Naldo to the kids. He too assumed the cannonball position and disappeared downwards into the abyss.

"Geronimo!" shouted the gnome. Instead of adopting the cannonball position he propelled himself into the middle by pushing with his feet and took on the position a parachutist would in free fall. His belly facing down, knees bent, arms outstretched, the skin on his face wobbling. "Belly flop. Coming down!" he shouted as he too disappeared into the void. Amazingly his hat stayed perched on his head as the children watched him disappear into a small dot.

Having carefully stowed away his Magigad, Sam edged his way around to Grace. There were just the two of them left. Sam grabbed Grace's hand. They looked nervously at each other. They both nodded, counted to three, they pushed off into the center, both tucking in their knees to their chins still holding hands tightly. In the tuck position, it was surprisingly easy to leave the wall. Grace resisted the urge to hold her nose, as they too plummeted downwards into the unknown.

Chapter 10

Tales of a Tooth Fairy

Darkness swirled around them, intertwined with occasional lights flashing. Grace and Sam could hear the others below making whooping noises to each other. It was probably only about thirty seconds falling, but it seemed much longer. Then suddenly, without warning there was a sensation of jumping into water. They even felt as though there was a splash, slightly taking their breath away and stopping their fall.

What had really happened was that they had hit a wave, but not a wave of water, a wave of air forcing up from beneath them. Just as if they had cannonballed into a pool, they sunk down into the air, then were shot back up by the wind, gradually the breeze from under them slowed leaving them levitating as though floating for a few seconds, until finally gravity gently returned them to the floor next to smiling Joel, Naldo and the belly flopping gnome. The air, not water, had broken their fall, but it had left them with the impression that they had plunged into the surface of a pool.

"Welcome to Port Enchantment," beamed Naldo. "Did you like the Airflush? You used to just land on a pile of sand until Geeko revamped it with the invention of the Airflush. I love that!!"

"Who is Geeko?" asked Grace breathlessly. She was still convinced she had plunged into a pool and had held her breath, but as she felt herself, she was surprised to find she was completely dry. Weird, she was pretty sure a porthole was a window on a ship, shouldn't they be wet? It certainly felt as though they were getting wet and an air flush? Was that like a flush of a toilet? Had they just jumped into a toilet? Then they should be wet. She was confused.

"Tis I," answered the gnome-looking-guy politely, answering the only question Grace had spoken aloud. He took off his hat and bowed low before them. He looked taller somehow.

"The Airflush worked pretty well again I must say!" He looked over his spectacles at the children. "It is still pretty new. I simply use the air, forced to the side through the centrifugal force. Diverted it down special tubes in the side of the Porthole and then back upwards to form a cushion. It took me a long time to work out a new ending. Landing in the sand was a pretty primal way to land. Causation of a few bruises ... But now the Airflush is a luxurious way to land and timed perfectly to push into the air to give the transformation stage time to work without any lag. Seamless almost." He continued, sounding like a TV commercial.

"I recently read a study in the Geomechanical Magic Magazine which said that air-flushing is the future of size transformation Magology. The air component can portion out the solution exactly, as it can adjust its solution according to the weight and height of the unique jet stream surrounding each person. It can also remember the exact adjustment for re-entry. Hey Naldo, Joel, do you remember how mad Pixel was when she ended up even smaller."

Naldo laughed "Oh my yes, she did get her tutu in a twist over that I thought she was going to explode. Good job you tweaked the Airflush. I wouldn't want the kids to see that. It was quite distressing."

"Yeah we have seen some Pixel drama in the past, but that was something. I thought she was going to get her pixie dust out and shrink you Geeko!" agreed Joel.

Joel continued with Geeko's story, "Then there was that time when metal didn't transform Naldo's cabin keys in his pockets didn't transform and were so heavy they made a hole in his shorts. Now that was hilarious." The memory made him chuckle.

"Buddy!" Naldo interrupted, "That was not hilarious, that was embarrassing. I had to literally drag the keys till we got to Aunt V, they were so heavy. No help from you guys!" He pointed at Joel and Geeko. "You were too busy laughing. I left the keys with Aunt Veronica but I basically had to keep my hand in my pocket all day to stop the hole getting any bigger and my pants literally ripping. I did not enjoy that day. Having to worry about your pants tearing apart was a total buzz killer." Naldo paused contemplatively, then continued "Dude ... imagine if your clothes didn't transform, just you ... Now that would be crazy."

"Crazy embarrassing for you!" continued Joel. "Luckily, I am so talented at towel folding that I could have done a little clothing origami then Baboom no problemo for me!" It was Joel's time to pause in contemplation. "Hey Geeko." Joel added. "How come our zippers didn't stay large? They are metal too. Now that would have been a complete disaster, it would pull your shorts down, even my superior clothing origami would not have saved me."

"Components of fabric combined with the B26 dispersed the effect of the metal ratio," answered Geeko. "The keys consist of total metal in a solid form, the B26 did not have a chance of changing its component. I had to consult with Professor Elk at the School of Magology to find a solution. Absolutely, amazingly clever gnome Professor Elk, very wise. As soon as the B26 was adjusted the problem was solved"

Grace and Sam had just begun to wonder if they would ever understand anything this strange Gnome said, when he directed his attention to them.

"What did you think of the experience Grace and Sam?" He looked them over carefully, "Seems to have worked perfectly for you both."

Before either Grace or Sam could reply, there was a gust of wind and a shadow came upon them. Grace squeezed closer to Sam.

A familiar voice said, "Hello, did you miss me?"

"Not really Pixel," answered Naldo, "You are always late. We sort of expect it."

"Hmphh," replied Pixel. Grace looked at her carefully, something was different, in comparison to before, she looked huge. She was not quite the same size as Sam, but she had definitely grown. Sam had obviously come to the same conclusion.

"Woah. You got so much bigger." Sam commented loudly, but suddenly remembering, maybe a little too late, that it was impolite to mention a girl's size. He corrected himself "I mean you got taller, not bigger obviously you are not fatter, I mean bigger. I mean taller.....yikes. I am just going to stop talking right now."

Pixel ignored Sam's stuttering over the definition of size. "Haven't you told them what just happened to them?" exclaimed Pixel. "You need to do that right now." She fluttered her wings. "I'm just so glad I get to skip around the transformation portion. You never know what it will do to my wing chitin."

Grace and Sam frowned. They were totally confused.

"Oh don't worry about 'that' Grace or Sam neither of you have scales made of chitin!" Naldo interrupted emphasizing the word scales. Pixel stuck her tongue out at him, "They are not scales." Pixel pouted, "Fish have scales. Snakes have scales. I do not have scales. I have beautiful wings with spectacular chitin. Chitin is my wing's amazing sheen." She added the last sentence for the kids' benefit.

"Pixel is really just jealous," Naldo interrupted again. "She has to skip the last part of the Airflush. The Airflush is the cool bit. The part when it feels as though you are landing in a pool. The awesome part."

Pixel was, as Naldo suggested, obviously a little miffed that she had to miss out on the Airflush, as she pouted even more.

After a short slightly uncomfortable pause, Grace broke the silence. "Oh, I wasn't landing in a pool? I wondered why I wasn't wet." She ran her hand again over her sleeve as though to check she still was not wet now.

Geeko temporarily ignored Grace. He directed his attention to the pouting Pixel; her wings were flapping furiously at Naldo. Naldo stared back, obviously amused by it all.

"Pixel," started Geeko diplomatically, "I've told you before. I am so sorry you can't do the end bit. The sensation of falling into water is certainly fun, but it is simply a bonus side effect of both forces of air and the potion meeting. The air from one's fall hits against the air I designed to flush up to meet you through the porthole pipes. It is best that you don't try, as it is a little shocking and you are right it may affect the wing chitin. You do have the most beautiful sheen to your wings."

Pixel blushed and looked happier, having received Geeko's compliment. Her wings fluttered slower and she did look majestic. Her wings glistened like morning snow. But her smile faltered as Geeko continued.

"Eventually I want to tweak it so the last part creates a sensation of falling through water then a fun swirl like you are tubing. It will be so incredible. Like an amazing water park ride"

He was obviously someone who liked to express himself by his hand gestures, as he had been waving his arms around during his speech so much that he had almost knocked Pixel over. "Sorry," he motioned to Pixel. "I do love waterparks." His arms flailed around and he made sound effects as though he was sliding down a huge water slide.

A little too late, he noticed Pixel's expression had returned to a pout of disapproval, as she realized that she would never experience the fun of the waterslide. Geeko hastily retracted his last statement, "But I may just tweak it to a more calm, less adventurous fall."

While Geeko was talking, Sam suddenly had a vision of Geeko dressed like the gnome in the adverts, the one who traveled around the world. In his vision, Geeko was dressed in swimming trunks and a very loud Hawaiian shirt, climbing the stairs to the tube slide with everyone else but instead of a tube, Geeko had a surfboard under his arm and was half the size of everyone else. Sam was not sure why in his vision Geeko would be carrying a surfboard up the tube slide. Sam shook his head. Human frogs and surfing gnomes. His imagination was going crazy. He tried to return to the conversation.

"I loved it, Geeko," said Sam, "Don't change it!" Grace, Naldo and Joel nodded in agreement. "Or maybe, change it to add the waterslide part," whispered Joel under his breath so Pixel could not hear him. Grace snorted loudly trying not to laugh, then tried to cover up her snort with a cough, and a hiccup which caused all four of them to laugh. Pixel glared at them all fully aware she was the reason for their mirth.

Geeko ignored them all and continued on. "Well, I love it as well, but it may be a little adventurous for the older or younger magical folk. Even some fairies might have trouble, they would have to be agile, like Pixel, to jump left before the air flush so as not to damage their wings. I need to redesign an optional gentler landing and they can all come the same way. Hmmm," he raised his hand to his chin thinking, after a brief pause he carried on talking. "Pixel you are right. We'd better explain the porthole to Grace and Sam. And fill them in on why we are here?"

"This is Geeko's invention," explained Naldo proudly, "It allows magical folks to move around the world from one magical land to another. Using cruise ships as their portal."

"Fairies, elves and pixies can get around pretty well with their wings. That is as long as they are old enough and not too old to fly long distances," continued Pixel. Glad to change the subject from her inability to join in the fun through the Airflush.

"But very young or older pixies, elves, fairies, as well as gnomes and other magical folk without wings, can't travel around the world easily. All magical folk love to travel and visit foreign friends and families just like humans. Geeko had realized there was an opportunity and invented a way to use the cruise lines. That is how I met up with Reynaldo and Joel. A year ago, I was still young and having trouble with my flying. We needed to see my Great Grandma in Brazil, as she was sick. My Mom and Dad heard about the invention Geeko was installing and they took me to the Brilldom.

Well, I am pretty curious, so one night I overheard my parents talking to an older pixie lady, explaining that the portal started in the laundry room and long story short, I went looking for the portal and ended up in the staff quarters. In fact to be exact, I ended up not in the laundry room but in Naldo and Joel's sleeping quarters and after they tried to stamp on me thinking I was a large bug, they were very nice." She glared at Naldo and Joel. "Well maybe not quite as apologetic as they might have been but nice enough ... I was actually very lucky. I have since found out that not everyone is as nice to fairy folk; some humans would have continued stomping on me or even worse. Some humans have this idea to capture magical folk and make their fortune showing them off in cages. Along with other horrible ideas. Experimentation, exploitation ... " She shuddered.

"Naldo and Joel looked after me and kept me hidden. Mom and Dad had realized pretty fast that I was missing and sent out Geeko who came to get me and took me back to the safe area."

"You can't blame us for freaking out a little and not apologizing straight away," Joel mentioned, "This busy, buzzy flying thing was zooming around our room and when we tried to swat it, as we did we heard it shout at us."

"In an ear piercing tone," Naldo added, "I am surprised no one came running into the room thinking the fire alarm had gone off. Pixel is amazingly loud for a little one."

"I was not so loud," insisted Pixel.

"Yes you were," contradicted Naldo, "I thought it was some kind of death moth which deafened it's prey before eating it little by little. You can't blame us. We are raised to believe that fairies and magical stuff are the subjects of children's bedtime stories, not real. We were obviously long, long past thinking they were real. Right kids?" Naldo motioned to Grace and Sam, who raised their eyebrows and nodded in agreement. Fairies, pixies, elves and gnomes had not been real to them for a long time now. That was until now when one, no, actually two, magical folk, a fairy or pixie thing and a gnome thing had appeared before them.

Pixel ignored Naldo's commentary about the noise and continued her story, "So, Naldo and Joel became friends with Geeko. Asking him all sorts of questions when he came to take me back to my parents. Geeko was so flattered about their interest, that he showed them his invention and let them enter the portal. He even made the entrance big enough for them to get through and join in the fun. They even get to go through the Airflush. They were the only humans ... that is until you two came along. You kind of gatecrashed actually. Were you ever given permission?" She motioned to Grace and Sam, who tried not to look guilty. Then she went back to reminiscing.

"Well as a youngster, I came back through the Portal many times. I loved traveling so much. I asked to be stationed on one and I was lucky enough to be put on this boat as the resident tooth fairy. I already knew my way around and was very competent. Did you know 17% of kids between the ages of 4 and 12 years old lose their teeth on vacation? 8.7 % of that 17% on cruises. I am not sure why, maybe it's all the sugary things on the buffet? Anyhow, Joel and Naldo help me find the right child's cabin without bumping into the humans, especially those who want to put us in a cage.

You have no idea how hard it is to be a tooth fairy on a cruiseliner. Punters or passengers as you call them are up all the time, every hour of the day. The corridors are so narrow and low it is hard to stay hidden. The windows of the cabins don't open. They are reinforced against bad weather and some cabins don't even have windows! Ponder cruises have six or seven tooth fairies, but I am alone. I do love all the adventure and danger though ! I have become super creative." She paused for a breath, "Plus, the days we are in port are so much fun! I have to deliver the teeth to the local tooth depot, then we can do some sightseeing. "

"Pixel enough talking, we need to get going. Stick close kids" said Joel. "We will explain more later."

Chapter 11

Aunt Veronica's Cookies

The kids followed the strange group through a doorway. "Pixel and Geeko have definitely grown," thought Sam. It was a little unnerving. Maybe he was imagining it. No, they were nearly the same height as him now. Weird. The door led to another room decorated with framed artwork and tropical plants. In the far corner sat a motherly looking gnome behind a desk, knitting what looked like a bright purple scarf, an eggplant purple. She obviously likes purple. Her pointed hat was purple and her shirt a purple and white stripe with a fashionable collar and a matching purple skirt. A lot of purple but it suited her. She smiled widely, looking over her glasses, when she saw them. Her smile was particularly broad when Geeko stopped at her desk. Her knitting needles clicked faster.

"Morning Aunt V.," Geeko smiled back. "Is everything working well? "

"That is Mrs Veronica, Geeko's Aunt," whispered Naldo to Grace, "She is half gnome and half witch, she can fix anything and makes a wickedly good apple pie! Or should I say, witchedly good apple pie!' He laughed, "Make sure to say 'yes' if she ever asks you home for dinner. But don't eat the chocolate chip cookies if you can help it. She likes everyone to call her Aunt V."

Grace had lots of questions about Aunt Veronica, but it seemed rude to ask them, especially while Geeko and Aunt V. were talking.

"Everything is working just fine. You worry too much Geeko. Hello Joel, Hello Reynaldo, Hello Pixel, love. How is your Mother?" asked Aunt Veronica looking fondly at them all.

"Very well Aunt V.," replied Pixel cheerfully, "I dropped off the Trackle cover you knitted her last time I was home. She said to give you this." She twitched her shoulders and a parcel dropped from between her wings. She caught it with amazing accuracy and passed it to Aunt V.

"Oh my!" exclaimed Aunt V. excitedly, unwrapping the brown wrapping paper in haste. A small silvery square shaped stone dropped out. "Oh the Sudoku Stone 5000. I am going to have so much fun with this. Please thank her Pixel. She is such a dear. I shall have to hurry up with my knitting so you can have something to take back. I was thinking of ear plug covers for her noise canceling earbuds?" She held up the purple wool to show Pixel.

"Beautiful" said Pixel admiringly "She will love it!!"

"Aunt Veronica and my Mom went to M.F.C (Magical Folk College) together," whispered Pixel to the children. "They are always swapping presents. Aunt V likes to knit everything, my Mom loves the stuff, but Joel and Naldo have a bet to see when she will run out of ideas and send Mom a knitted toilet paper holder. Apparently by the way they laugh a knitted toilet paper holder is a very funny human gift. They were all excited when last Christmas Aunt V. gifted Mom a knitted cover for her tissues. They have been disappointed ever since.

Aunt V. seems to have gone techno. My mom works in the Magology Innovation Department of the coalition. She gets Aunt V the latest technological presents in the Magic Folk World. The Sudokia Stone is the latest craze for Folk over 100 years old. It combines Sudoku with Trivia. It's a bit boring for us young ones. But Aunt V. loves that stuff. Look at her glasses. They have a switch on them that turns her glasses into a virtual reality headset. She can use them to see anywhere in the Muffle. The Magical Folk Local, MLK or Muffle. That is where we are now, or nearly. I don't think she will ever make a knitted toilet paper cover. She is way too cool now."

Grace and Sam were very appreciative that Pixel explained the confusing acronyms and slang into terminology they could vaguely understand.

"Of course now I have the new Sudokia Stone 5000. It might take a little longer," Aunt V. continued, as she patted the stone appreciatively. "It is going to be hard to think of knitting when I could be playing with my amazing new toy."

"Much traffic today Aunt V?" asked Geeko, changing the subject.

"I certainly have had a busy day," replied Aunt V. cheerily, "27 ticketed Magical Folks, 3 unicorns and a rabbit. They all loved the new Airflush. We are expecting 32 more to board tonight including the Italian and Irish National Pearlball teams. Who are you new friends?"

"How rude of me. This is Grace," Geeko motioned in the direction where Grace was standing. "And this is Sam," he waved over flamboyantly towards Sam.

"Hello Grace. I love your hair." Grace was always getting compliments about her hair. "Bigger than Texas" muttered Sam to Naldo, who laughed. Aunt V. leant over the desk and shook Grace's hand heartily.

"Hello Sam love," she said, shaking his hand too. She paused, staring at them for a moment. "Are you twins?" Grace groaned and Sam grinned broadly.

"No, ma'am. We are not twins." said Sam, still chuckling.

Grace and Sam were almost the same height, even though Grace was two and a half years older. It used to be just on an odd occasion that someone would ask if they were twins but it had become more and more common, much to Grace's chagrin. "I'm older," said Grace a little, but not too sulkily, "Two years 7 months older actually. Three whole school grades." She wanted to make the point very clear that she was in fact older and in her opinion way smarter.

"Oh, of course," consoled Aunt V., sensing this was a little bit of a sore point for Grace. "Maybe Geeko can adjust the Shrinking

Station and make Grace just a wincey bit taller than Sam when you go back through the Airflush."

"*Shrinking Station*," thought Grace, "*I haven't been through a shrinking station.*" But then she realized that Sam, Reynaldo, Joel and herself were all the same height as Pixel and Geeko. Or at least they all had similar dimensions. Joel and Naldo were still taller than Grace and Sam and Pixel was still the smallest. But either Pixel and Geeko had grown or Grace, Sam, Naldo and Joel had shrunk.

Sam had listened carefully too. 'Shrinking station', he knew he hadn't imagined that Pixel and Geeko had seemed larger. But he had had it the wrong way around, the humans had shrunk. He felt a bit of panic twist in his stomach.

Grace obviously had come to the same conclusion and was feeling a similar sensation. "When did that happen?" Grace stuttered, "And why didn't we notice....ermm... feel it earlier? We are smaller?"

Sam was examining his hands and moving his feet in all directions, as though testing everything still worked. It looked terribly funny, like a strange, wobbly, robotic dance. Sam looked up, sensing everyone was watching him, he went bright red and stopped the dance immediately.

"Excellent moves dude" laughed Joel and mimicked Sam perfectly adding a kind of electronic drumming noise to the actions.

Even Sam had to laugh.

When Geeko stopped laughing, he answered the children's questions in turn, starting with Sam's unasked one.

"Don't worry Sam as your dance showed us, you are still in perfectly good working order." Joel continued with the electronic drumming sound in the background.

"I added an optional 'Shrinking Station' to the Airflush to accommodate my good friends, Naldo and Joel. This allows them to enjoy the magical world in full without attracting too much attention. Or more importantly crushing any of our more delicate magical members or crashing through the ceiling of the MFL," he added. "The feature is actually located within the Airflush. As you felt that diving under the water sensation and then the feeling of rising up before you landed on your feet. That is when it actually happened. I pride myself that it is such a smooth transition that you can hardly notice. It took Joel well over an hour to notice he had shrunk the first time."

It was Joel's turn to blush this time. He promptly stopped the background drumming noise and grinned sheepishly. "It's true," he admitted.

Geeko continued, "It is natural to take a while to realize. There have been so many other stimuli that it takes a while for all the senses to catch up. Some 'sense' takes longer than others." He glanced mischievously over at Joel who shrugged his shoulders smiling at everyone. "Pixel and I always take a detour so we are actually our usual size. I did test it out a few times though. Awesome sensation I must say."

Pixel rose in the air and twirled around. "That was what I was trying to explain. I have not been allowed to experience the 'awesome sensation of the new airflush'. I miss all the fun."

"I just don't want to ruin your fabulous, beautiful wing chitin Pixel," placated Geeko. "Don't worry though, Grace and Sam," continued Geeko to the children. "You all will be back to normal height by the time you return to the ship. Everything is recorded in detail and potion quants already allocated. Back in a sec."

Geeko disappeared through a door on the left.

Aunt V. opened a drawer behind the desk and pulled out a cookie jar.

"Would either of you like a cookie? They are chocolate chip or raisin cinnamon? They are good for a shock."

Sam felt suddenly hungry; it had been a long time since his epic breakfast. "Yes please" he said eagerly and reached across the desk into the jar taking his favorite cookie (chocolate chip).

Grace remembered Naldo's warning about the chocolate chip cookies, but also felt hungry and reached into the jar taking the raisin cinnamon instead. She thought about warning Sam but decided there was no polite way to do that. What if Naldo had been joking? Then that would seem rude, she didn't want to offend Aunt

V. Plus, she was still a little mad about how happy Sam had looked after being called a twin.

Sam bit with relish into the cookie which smelt delicious. A strange sensation ran through his tongue, the cookie had turned into a liquid. It made his tongue tingle, but had the wonderful taste of a smooth hot chocolate. Then the chocolate turned into lemonade, then root beer, oddly to broccoli then fuzzed like sweet sherbet and disappeared. It was not unpleasant, just a little startling and made Sam's face contort into all kinds of different shapes. Especially as the taste turned unexpectedly to broccoli.

Naldo and Joel had been closely watching Sam's reaction, they had obviously all had the same reaction at some point. They laughed and patted his shoulder. "Magical taste Aunt V.'s cookies. Right Sam" Naldo giggled. Sam, being a good sport, immediately smiled and took another bite. It actually was fun when you knew the sensations and tastes change. In fact when he thought about it, the tastes were all of Sam's favorite tastes. It was just a little shocking as you expected a chocolate chip cookie to taste like chocolate chip cookies and the tastes changed so fast it was hard to keep up.

"Magical," confirmed Sam.

Grace, still laughing at Sam's silly facial expressions, took a huge bite of her raisin cinnamon cookie, so glad that she had been warned about the chocolate chip cookies. She did not see Reynaldo to her left trying to attract her attention. He was mouthing "Same thing," trying to tell her that all the cookies had strange tastes too, but she didn't see him.

She had not been chewing the cookie for long when she realized that she too had a unique cookie.

The first raisin had been perfectly normal, sweet and cinnamony, the second tasted as sour as an airhead. Before she could get used to it, the cookie batter turned into cheese pizza, then tortilla chips, then back to cookie dough and finally to kiwis and lime before it too melted away like ice cream on a hot day.

Grace's expressions were obviously even funnier than Sam's, as everyone including Sam roared with laughter. Only Reynaldo and Aunt V. remained quiet.

"Sorry I should have mentioned the raisin cookies too," Naldo noted apologetically.

"Aunt V.," scolded Geeko, returning to the room and seeing everyone's faces "You really have to stop offering out those surprise cookies. Or at least you should warn people."

"Oh Geeko," Aunt V. reasoned. "The very essence of the recipe is 'surprise'. That is why they are called 'surprise cookies'. They are programmed to allow you to taste all of your favorite tastes in one perfect cookie dough. I think they are a great idea. All your favorite culinary delights in one place. Incidentally, they are much better than the first ones Reynaldo and Joel tried. I accidentally reversed the recipe and the cookie had all the person's least liked tastes instead of their favorites. That was a surprise."

Reynaldo and Joel looked at each other and nodded. Obviously judging by their expressions it had been bad.

With that confession, Aunt V. took out a cookie and bit into it enthusiastically. " Mmmmm brownies " she murmured with her mouthful "mmmm feta cheese, mmmm clam chowder, mmmm tiramisu ..." She swallowed, "Okay maybe the sweet/salty combo is a little strange." Her face contorting just like Grace and Sam's faces had, into weird shapes as the tastes changed. Everyone laughed this time including Aunt V. Aunt V. offered the plate around to the others who eagerly took one describing the tastes as they arrived, even Grace and Sam took a second one.

"Enough chat and cookie talk. Where can I send you to?" interrupted Aunt V. eventually.

"Quick stop at the International Tooth Depot for Pixel to unload, then up to the MLF Enchantment Lodge if you would please," replied Geeko grabbing another surprise cookie and performing his own contorted mouth dance as the tastes changed for him again.

"Certainly Sir G," said Aunt V., saluting. She tapped her knitting needle onto the desk. The needles immediately changed into two wands. She pointed one at the door and muttered some words to herself. The door opened and revealed a rather plush looking elevator. They all piled in; there was ample room.

Geeko pushed some buttons; the door closed and the elevator moved smoothly upwards. They could hear Aunt V. shouting, "Cheerio," as they ascended.

Grace could not help but feel a rush of excitement as the numbers counting the floors rushed by. They really were having an adventure.

Soon, the elevator came to a stop. Pixel fluttered her wings out of her back and pressed a button to open the door.

"Back in 5," she giggled. The door opened and the children got a brief glance revealing a brightly lit foyer. Pixel winked as she flew out. The doors closed promptly.

"Pixel loves the fact we cannot go in," grumbled Naldo. "Those tooth fairies love all the secrecy about what happens to the children's teeth they collect. I am so curious. She loves to wind me up about it."

"Not even other magical folk get let in on the secret," explained Geeko patiently. "We are not even allowed out on this floor. They say if we all knew what went on, the magic would be lost. The rumor is that they crush it into a powder and use it to sprinkle on children having bad dreams so that they can have good dreams instead. Some say that the tooth fairies are double agents, they collect teeth and they carry around magical dream changing powder so they can stop bad dreams as they move around. Another rumor is they have a secret compartment in their wing pouch which they rub on the tooth powder to help them fly. Yet another is the power to ..."

"I think they just want to be ... oh so secret," interrupted Naldo moodily. He then smiled his bright smile again and the children wondered if he was really upset or just joking with them.

Chapter 12

Muffles and Trackles

Pixel returned with a huge smile. "All done," she winked provocatively at Naldo, who stuck out his tongue childishly then smiled back.

The doors closed and the elevator moved silently upwards.

"So now where are we going?" asked Grace.

"The Enchanted Lodge" answered Reynaldo with an excited look on his face. "The MFL for this port. It is like a hotel but for magical folk. It provides them with a safe place to stay while they are traveling."

"Wow, are we below the earth's crust?" asked Grace, remembering her science lessons and what Reynaldo had told them back in the moss room.

"Yep" answered Naldo " Between the lithosphere and the asthenosphere. We could not fit in our usual size."

"Time for a PAA, a Potentially Amazing Adventure," mused Sam, "That is an acronym, Grace. An abbreviation formed by the initial components in a phrase or word. In case you forgot. Like BENELUX" He giggled knowing this would embarrass her.

It was Grace's turn to stick out her tongue.

Geeko had not noticed the sibling joke and continued explaining the history of the MFL. "It is not easy for us magical folk to find a safe hiding place these days. Especially in an unfamiliar place. Almost every port has a Magical Folk Local (MFL) affectionately called a Muffle. This port's Muffle is named the Enchanted Lodge. A Muffle does much more than provide a safe place for magical folk to rest and to sleep, they can pick up their Trackles to help find safe spots in the area. A Trackle is similar to a GPS or navigation system but not only does it show how to get somewhere fast, it shows us how to get somewhere fast without being spotted by humans. Finds us places where we can be together safely, unnoticed by humans and other predators. It can even link magical folk up with local friendly animals and birds to help with transportation."

Seeing the kid's confused expression, he went to continue further. But he was interrupted by Pixel.

"My grandma still prefers to use an old fashioned map. But then she is a little quirky."

She twiddled on her bracelet and out popped a screen the size of a quarter on her wrist. It looked a little like a slightly oversized watch. She pressed on it a few times and showed everyone a picture of her grandma. Sam was impressed with all the magical world technology. An hour ago, he would have laughed at anyone saying that magical folk existed. Now he was marveling at their advancements since the fairy tales he had heard as a small child.

Pixel's grandma looked exactly like Pixel. She had the same smile and even the same mischievous glimmer in her eye. The only difference was that unlike Pixel, she was wearing the clothes which children's literature might lead you to expect a fairy to wear. A shimmering pale pink dress which looked as though it could be made of rose petals and matching rose petals in her hair. In contrast, Pixel was in very modern clothes, a sequined T-shirt and jeans.

When Sam saw the photo he asked Pixel, "Wow. Was your Grandma your age when the photo was taken? You look so alike."

Pixel laughed, "Woah. You two really have no idea about fairy folk do you? My grandma is 167 years old. Fairies don't age like humans. You probably think Geeko is super old, don't you?"

"He is not old?" asked Sam, confused. He took a closer look at Geeko. He did look old, old like you always see gnomes in books. But on closer examination his clothes were very up to date and trendy, the colors you would expect a gnome to wear: bold green, red and blue. But his blue pants had a trendy cut with embroidery on the pockets, his T-shirt had the words 'Geeky and Proud' written on it in swirly writing.

Sure, he had a red garden gnome-like hat, but if you looked closely it had a small unfamiliar logo printed all over it, making it look cool. It also had a small ridge on the front like a mini baseball hat peak, where he had balanced his trendy looking sunglasses. On examination his eyes looked very youthful, it was maybe only his stature which made him look old.

"How old are you both then?" Grace asked Pixel, looking just as confused as Sam.

"I am nineteen. And Geeko is twenty eight." answered Pixel, her laughter vibrating around the elevator sounding a little like a wind chime on a breezy day.

She paused, "So actually Sam, you are right. To us young ones, Geeko is indeed really, really old."

"Ha ha" said Geeko in a monotone voice, "Remarkable invention the Trackle." He continued ignoring Pixel's joke and Grace and Sam's ignorance about the magical folk world. "Wish I had invented it," Geeko sighed distractedly.

After a pause, Reynaldo continued, realizing Geeko was in his own world, imagining he invented the Trackle. So Reynaldo took on the job of educating Grace and Sam on the Trackle's qualities.

"The Trackle is different to a navigation device you might find on your phone or in your car. Magical folk cannot own their own personal one and pack them with them when they travel. There are a couple of reasons for this. You cannot buy the Trackle, the 'Enchantment Alliance' who are the elected officials of the Magical World, voted to make it accessible to all magical folk. It was voted that it simply would not be fair if only the rich could get the benefit of knowing how to stay safe. Everyone should have an equal opportunity therefore, Trackles cannot be bought but they are available to everyone.

This was a great decision; especially as Geeko said, things are not as they used to be, there are far fewer undisturbed woods or natural areas where magical folk can settle and make their home, very few places to live and relax in. Also, in the human world there are so many security devices now, burglar alarms, webcams and other devices that are so sensitive they can actually sense magical folk and get them in all kinds of trouble or just prevent them from going places. Ever heard an alarm go off for no apparent reason? Well, there's your answer, they located magical folk.

Suddenly your security camera goes dead for a second. Or your WiFi drops for no reason. Well some poor Magical Folk had to use their Trackle to reset your system to avoid you seeing them. Very irritating and time consuming for them.

Then there is the fact that there are so many more cars and planes around and they are so much faster! Making it almost impossible for folk to cross roads or flight paths. Life is much harder for magical folk to survive in and the Trackle makes it easier to navigate. Clever alliance members adapt it to change with all the technological advancements that us humans invent, steering the magical folks around danger and allowing them to go on with their business.

Technological advancements are another reason why the Trackle cannot be bought by an individual. Each Trackle needs to be returned to the central system every now and then to keep each one updated.

Each Trackle must be monitored in case the bad guys, 'the Weavers', get hold of it. MFLs - Muffles like the Enchanted Lodge are the central system, an amazing system; they make sure your Trackle is up to date and can tell the Enchanted Alliance, i.e. the good guys, if the Weavers, alias the bad guys, are getting close to any secret place or Muffle. We have to be careful, the Weavers also have great technology. They really want to get hold of a Trackle but the system does a great job of staying ahead. Each time one is checked out they use a fingerprint locking system to open it, but the Weavers are smart and they are getting close to being able to unlock one."

"Who are the Weavers and why do they want to harm the magical folk? " asked Sam.

"They are humans," answered Geeko simply. "Humans who have discovered that magical folk really exist. We are not entirely sure why they want to harm us, but we think we know why. The theory is they are trying to capture us, especially fairies and pixies so they stay looking young despite their age. As Reynaldo and Pixel just explained, these magical folk stay looking young their whole lives. Humans are obsessed about staying young and the Weavers want to examine the poor fairies, elves and pixies in order to find the secret of staying young and living forever. They think if they capture this secret formula, they can sell it to humans who want to stay youthful and make lots of money! Of course they cannot spread the word yet as so many of you think we are not real and no one would believe them. These humans fear age and they fear being thought stupid. So they want to capture us. Experiment on us, especially the winged ones and then reveal our existence to the world," Geeko shuddered.

Sam and Grace nodded; they both knew that lots of humans would pay a lot of money to keep their youthful looks and they wouldn't care where the product came from.

Naldo chimed in, looking directly at Pixel, "Another rumor is that the fairies use the children's teeth to keep themselves young and beautiful. Maybe it's the teeth that the Weavers are after. That is why they keep everything so secretive. They don't want to share. "

"Pah," responded Pixel, "if that was the case I would certainly smuggle some out to put on your ugly, old face Naldo. So I don't have to look at it being so old and ugly all the time." She smiled fondly to let him know she was joking but remained smug that she had had such a fast and funny retort.

Naldo was about to reply, but the elevator stopped. They had arrived and Grace and Sam could not wait to see the Enchanted Lodge.

Chapter 13

The Enchanted Lodge

As the doors opened the kids got their first look into the magical world in front of them. The lodge looked like a very modern hotel. It was very minimalistic and very white!

The carpet was white, the sofas were white, the walls were painted white. Large televisions were mounted at regular intervals on the white walls and there were huge silver desks in each corner. Every now and then there was a very modern photo of nature close up hung on the wall. Huge dandelion seeds were featured on one and magnified pictures of shells in beautiful pastel on another. The photos were so clear they almost looked 3D.

Grace was particularly taken by the shell picture. She marveled at how interesting the shell's texture and colors looked up close. Sam, however, was not looking at the decor. He was fascinated by the strange and wonderful people he could see. He still could not believe that magical folk existed. Of course, he had been spending the main part of his day with a fairy, a gnome and oh yes the gnome's aunt. But these were fictional right? Maybe it still was all a dream? Or a hologram?

So, what do you do if you think you are in a dream? Yes, he reverted to the old, tried and tested method to check if you are dreaming he pinched himself. Ouch! It hurt. He was not dreaming. Also, he concluded, no dream of his could really be this strange. These were not the magical folk you see in children's books; there was no way his weak imagination could not come up with all this. Nope, he was not dreaming.

He spotted what he thought were Leprechauns. Yes, they were all in the traditional green but they were wearing baseball hats and team T-shirts with four leaf clover logos. These were not the rainbow/gold chasing leprechauns he read about in books.

"That is some of the Irish national Pearlball team." swooned Pixel as the Leprechauns walked by. She sounded slightly star struck, "They were the champions last year." She pushed them towards a table filled with delicious treats. Sam looked at her with a pathetic hungry look. "It is no trick. Aunt V was not involved in the preparation of this food," she laughed, "Just delicious food." She offered Grace and Sam a plate and they began savoring the delights in front of them. Magically delicious, but thankfully normal food. Geeko, Naldo and Joel followed suit and grabbed a pile of food.

"Another bonus of the Muffle," spluttered Joel, his mouthful of food. "Delicious, free food. There are always free samples."

There were also many magical folk with wings. Geeko explained, between munching, that winged magical folk were affectionately named fairy folk and the elves and pixies didn't seem to mind.

The fairy folk were all chatting together merrily with the same beautiful sing song voice that Pixel had. They were dressed in the trendy clothes you might expect to see in a high school or a teen at a rock concert. The only difference to high school students or concert goers was that they had delicate wings sticking out from their backs. Some even had backpacks especially formed to fit and store their wings just like Pixel. Each of the fairy folk wings seemed to have a different glow. What was the word Pixel used? A different chitin. Some wings glowed gold and silver, others like moth wings silky and delicate, a few were like hummingbird colors; metallic and shimmery. Each set of wings were beautiful, in a subtle, yet different way.

Gnomes were smaller and stouter than fairy folk but just as trendy. Some wore suits, carried leather suitcases or small briefcases and looked very important. Others were dressed like pop stars or models. Strangely, every now and then a magical animal would walk by: Unicorns, phoenix, owls and even regular animals like rabbits or squirrels, walking on their hind legs, carrying bags and chattering to each other. Oddly, every animal was a similar size; the rabbit was as tall as the unicorn, the owl the same height as the phoenix. "That must be the Airflush" decided Sam. Both Sam and Grace could have stayed there all day, magical folk spotting. It was fascinating.

"Let's go get our Trackles," said Geeko.

Sam was easily redirected. He was equally fascinated by the thought of viewing a new gadget, as he was by the magical creatures. What exactly was a Trackle? What would it look like? How would it work? His stomach buzzed with excitement. The same excitement he felt on the release date of a new update or game for his Magigad.

They all followed Geeko over to one of the silver desks. A pretty looking elf came over, her hair was a deep brown and swept back in a tight bun. She had bright red lipstick and wore a white suit with a familiar logo on her lapel. Sam had seen this logo before. He soon figured out where. It was the same logo that was printed all over Geeko's gnome hat.

"Hello," the elf greeted them. "How are you all today? Welcome to the Enchanted Lodge. We are at the Italian port. Are you exploring the outer land today? Or staying in the lodge? We have Trackles set ready to go. If you are exploring the outer land, there is lots of excitement going on. You may have seen some of the fans and teams arriving; this afternoon is the first Pearlball competition of the season. It will be moving on with the Brilldom tomorrow to Greece. Are you planning on attending the game? I can program your Trackle to get you straight there if you like? Or would you rather go to the local tourist sights?"

She paused to look at the screen on her desk. "We are also offering the Magical Vineyard Tour, leaving in half an hour and led by our local Wizarding Ministry. There are award winning wine potions to be sampled. Cheese sampling is happening in the east wing right here at the Enchanted lodge. Or if you have more time the famous rock band 'The Pizza Pixies' are touring the local dough making depot at one o'clock. That tour includes samples of the top pixie chefs' pizza recipes."

Even though she had just eaten a large amount of delicious food from the buffet, Grace's mouth was beginning to water at the thought of pizza. But, Pixel had other ideas that could not contain her excitement any longer. "Oh, I would love to see the match," she cooed. "But we don't have tickets. Are all the tickets sold out?"

The elf pressed a few buttons on her screen. "Standing room only," she reported still smiling, "But, I do still have some tickets if you decide to go."

Pixel turned to Grace and Sam.

"I don't expect that you know what Pearlball is? Do you?" She didn't wait for an answer. "It is a wonderful sport which unites all magical folk. There are eleven folk in a team. Teams must consist of at least three different magical folk types and they must originate from the same country. This ensures the country works together, as friends and as a team. Some might be fairies, gnomes, leprechauns or unicorns, elves and pixies. It doesn't matter, but there has to be a mix. The ball is a pearl. So it is not perfectly round and it bounces off and rolls at different angles. Pearls and Oyster shells are also the only natural substances which are magic proof, so no one can even be tempted to cheat and use magic to bewitch the Pearlball or Oyster goal in their teams favor. So clever."

"Naldo and I went once. The Oystershell goals are amazing," continued Joel. "There are four of them on each side. They open and close so the shooters have to time their shot and choose the right shell at the right moment. But they only have twenty seconds to shoot once they step or fly into the Chuckdome. "

"What teams are playing today?" asked Sam curiously. He was beginning to think he might like to go and watch. Already sounded more fun than cricket or at least less rules.

"It is Italy versus England tonight," exclaimed Pixel excitedly. "I would love to see it. My friend Stryker is playing for England. We went to Tooth Fairy school together. She is super fast in the Chuckdome. The highest scorer in the UK last year. Let's go guys. I am sure Stryker could get us an upgrade from standing room only to seats."

She looked around to gauge the other's opinion. They all nodded eagerly. "You get us all tickets and Trackles, and I'll give Stryker a call," Pixel stepped away from the desk and took a small earpiece from her pocket and began chatting quietly to what seemed to be herself, but must have been to her friend Stryker.

The pretty elf behind the desk was waiting patiently. "Apparently, we would like to get tickets to the Pearlball tournament." Geeko informed her. "Oh I overheard," commented the Elf changing her voice to a whisper, "Do you think you could get Stryker's autograph for me? She is so awesome...I'm not really supposed to ask but ..."

Before she could finish her sentence. Pixel rejoined them. "Stryker says she can totally get us pitch side seats. Apparently the band 'Magical Fairyland' and 'The Pizza PIxies' are playing at the interval. Stryker says we can meet them all after the match! Come on we have to get a wiggle on to get there on time. "

"Okay," said the elf, "let's get you signed in for your Trackles and on your way. "Who is first?"

"We will get you autographs," stated Geeko confidently. "Pixel has no problem asking for things as you have noticed."

The elf laughed.

One by one Geeko, Pixel, Joel and Naldo stepped forward and put their hand on a hand shaped pad on the desk. Out popped a rod with some glasses attached to it. One by one they looked through the glasses, and a green light flashed. When it was Grace and Sam's turn, Grace went first putting her hand on the pad and a red light shone. The elf came over, frowning slightly. "Have you been registered yet?" she asked. Grace looked around at the others. Geeko shook his head.

"Ermm no," Grace answered nervously. Geeko stepped forward. "Sam and Grace are not yet in the system,' he explained. "Pixel and I will be their sponsors. This is their first visit, but we can vouch for their honesty."

The elf's smile returned. "Oh of course, then they will have to undergo the retina honesty scan and pureness test." She motioned to Grace and Sam to follow her through a door to a booth behind the desk. The children had to look through another set of glasses until a green light shone, then they entered one at a time into a glass tubular shaped container, a bit like the ones that security guards check you through at airports. A green light shone slowly around each of them, spiraling from their feet to their heads. There was a slight red glow when the light reached Sam's waist but then it glowed green again. Sam was worried about the 'pureness test' and whether it would note the incident of escaping the Busy and Fizzy Club, forging a sign out sheet, arguing with his sister ... the list of not pure actions he had committed, in the last twenty-four hours went on furiously in his head.

Luckily, after a couple of minutes the elf returned. "You both passed," she said cheerfully. "You have nothing but pure intentions to magical folk. The Pureness test was clear. But, I did see you have an unauthorized electronic gadget," she noted smiling at Sam. "I will just need to check the gadget, and confirm it is compatible with the Trackle's signals and won't hinder or impede the updates."

Sam took the Magigad 3000 out of his pocket. The elf opened it up, took a wand out of her pocket, tapped it twice then handed the Magigad back to Sam. "Cool," she said, "the Magigad 3000, I have always wanted to see one of those. Does it have an electrophon? "

"Oh yeah," replied Sam and just as he was just about to explain more a huge alarm sounded.

"Oh no," screeched the elf putting her hand to her mouth and rushing back to the desk. The children followed her, alarmed by her urgency.

"What's happening?" shouted Sam to Geeko over the sound of the alarm, magical folk were running back and forth looking frightened.

"A Trackle has been breached," shouted Geeko, looking at a screen above the elf's desk. The screen showed the words ``T-breach Code 1" in capital letters.

Geeko continued. "The Weavers have control of a Trackle. They can find out where the safe zones are. They can find magical folk. This is not good."

Chapter 14

The T-Breach Code 1

Panic broke out. Magical folk started swarming the desk, holding their Trackles up; others started to run or fly in all directions. Meanwhile, the alarm continued to ring loudly.

After what seemed like a long time but was probably less than a minute, the alarm sound changed into three short blasts after which everyone seemed to calm down and turn towards the television screens located around the lobby. The current screen which had been playing an interview with the Irish Pearlball team manager, flickered briefly then focused in on the face of a very distinguished yet worried looking gnome.

"That's Professor Elk," whispered Geeko in admiration. "He is the gnome who helped me with the airflush, inventor of the Trackle and chairman of the Magical Folk Coalition."

"*Busy man*," thought Grace.

Professor Elk was indeed a very impressive looking magical fellow, he was dressed in a suit with a tie but had a hat like a gnome sporting the same logo as Geeko's.

"This is a public safety announcement," Professor Elk said in a serious voice. "There is a T-Breach Code 1 underway. Our computers have alerted us that some of the security measures programmed into the Trackle devices have been breached. This means that they are no longer in secure mode. Any Trackle which gets into the wrong hands could now be used for wrongdoings by those inclined to hurt magical folk. It is our understanding that at least one Trackle has been stolen and is in the hands of the

Weavers. Furthermore, a Weaver has hacked into the system and can now see the location of all the Magical safe zones around the world."

There was a gasp from the crowd which had formed around the screen.

"For this reason, the Magical Coalition has decided to wipe all the Trackles clear of data. As each Trackle is accounted for by our team, it will be reset immediately with new encoded information. Until we have accounted for every Trackle and every one of our Magical Folk are accounted for, the security status will not be lowered." Professor Elk sighed, his brow frowning deeply. "The Coalition is fully aware that erasing all the Trackles will adversely affect many magical folk outside of a Muffle who are currently relying on the Trackle to guide them to safe zones. But the Coalition feels that this is the only way forward.

As stated, it is our understanding that at least one member of the Weavers is already in possession of a Trackle and our sources say that as we speak, the Weavers may be using it to find their way to the International Pearlball Competition. This information has yet to be confirmed, but, if it is indeed true, it would put a lot of magical folk in danger. Forty-five thousand Magical Folk have tickets and are heading to the stadium. We must stress, if you are in possession of a ticket do not leave the area. The game is canceled and our priority is to have everyone return safely. Including the the teams who are already at the stadium."

He paused as an intense looking gnome in a black suit and sunglasses appeared from the right of the screen. The gnome handed a note to Professor Elk who nodded and the gnome left. Professor Elk read the note and continued.

"All Trackles have all been successfully wiped of information."

There was a buzz almost in unison; folks all around, finding the source of the buzz, pulled out Trackles from their pockets and stared at them. Grace looked over the shoulder of a troll in front of her. The screen was blank but for the words 'T-Breach Code 1'. On the screen Professor Elk began to talk again.

"Before each Trackle device was simultaneously wiped clear of information, we put out a brief T-Breach Code 1 warning to everyone who has left a Muffle or Safe zone. We asked Folks to return calmly and vigilantly, to the nearest safe zone. The closest safe area to the Trackle was illuminated for four seconds before disappearing. Hopefully this gave them all enough time to note the location. But of course, this also means if a Weaver is indeed in possession of a Trackle, he or she will also have seen the location of the safe zone but only one safe zone.

For this reason, Coalition Security Squad members including trolls, witches, wizards, wolves, owls and their trained dragons have been sent to all safe zones in the area to monitor and safeguard the magical folk. In addition to the normal security practices, security will be intensified until the violation is under control.

We have also reached out to the animal kingdom to help us locate any stranded Magical Folk and assist them to the nearest safe zone. We are happy to report that the Animal Kingdom Trackle App has not been compromised and we are able to contact the registered Magic Folk's friendly animals, reptiles and insects freely. They of course as usual will be a great asset to our search and rescue mission.

Staff in safe zones and Muffles will be collecting and accounting for all Trackles. As the Trackles are returned, they will be encoded with new data allowing them to resume their usual missions safely again. We have been assured that the new code will be un-breachable, but it may take awhile to download. We ask for your patience and we ask that, unless it is a complete emergency, you stay in place until the breach is under control and our Coalition Security Squad have deemed it safe to leave.

Our staff are standing by at their desks to collect all the Trackles. Please proceed calmly and safely to the nearest desk to return yours. I repeat you are strongly advised to stay in the safe zone until further notice. For safety reasons, the portal entrance will remain closed to outgoing traffic until we get the all clear from the Coalition Security Squad.

On behalf of the Coalition of Magical Folks, thank you in advance for your cooperation. Please do not panic. Stay in the safe zone. We will keep you informed as soon as we have any further information. Rest reassured that the Coalition is and will do everything in its power to resume normal business and safeguard the Magical Folk's health and well being."

The screen switched back to the channel it had previously been playing except it looked as though the Irish Pearlball manager and his interviewer had left the building. The picture of the empty chair hazed over and the screen reset and began to play a previously recorded music program. Everyone in the lobby looked rather confused, but dutifully made their way over to the staff desk holding their Trackles.

The elf behind the desk had somehow transformed her desk into a larger desk. She no longer looked frightened and had been joined by a group of equally pretty elves and Fairy Folk who had started calmly collecting and scanning the Trackles then piling them on a back desk. Despite the fact there was a swarm of sad looking magical folk and animals around the desk, it was relatively calm. The elves reassured folk as they came up as though they were airport staff dealing with a flight cancellation.

Grace and Sam worked their way slowly through the crowd of Magical Folk heading towards the desk, following a subdued looking Geeko, Naldo and Joel. Pixel hovered nervously above their heads; her wings buzzing noisily. They found a white sofa in one of the corners, near the elevator door. The elevator they had used just a while ago to enter the Enchanted Lodge from the Portal now had a sign on it saying CLOSED and in front of the sign stood an official looking troll dressed in black.

Naldo broke the silence.

"Hmm, I see more than one problem here. Not only is the mere existence of the Magical World in jeopardy, but we cannot get back on the cruise ship. If the cruise ship moves on we will be stuck here until it is scheduled to return. If I remember rightly, that is in five months. I think we would have lost our jobs by then!," he said despondently. "Sorry to make this a human problem but... I'm just saying misery loves company."

Grace and Sam had not thought about this. It was true; if they could not get through the Portal, they could not get back up to the ship. The ship would leave without them and they would be left here. Sam had an idea.

"Couldn't we just go back up the gangway with the returning tourists? We could go out of the safe zone and walk around to the entrance. We can't be too far away. There must be some way out?" Sam suddenly felt much better and safer having found an answer.

"Oh Sam," Joel replied miserably, "if only it was that easy. There are two hurdles to your idea. "You do not have any documentation. The cruise ship security will not let you on without passports and tickets. "

Sam was unconvinced that this was an insurmountable problem. There must be a way they could get hold of their parents or maybe Joel and Naldo could vouch for them. Plus, they had bracelets from the Fizzy and Busy club; he looked down at his wrist. It wasn't there. It must have fallen off during their trip. Grace didn't have hers either.

"Oh and then," continued Joel sadly, as though he had been reading Sam's thoughts, "and more importantly, even if we could smuggle you in somehow, there is always the fact that we are all fairy-sized till we get back through the portal."

Sam sighed; he had forgotten that.

Grace felt panic rising in her chest. Much as she wanted to escape from the Brilldom, she did want to go home at some stage. She had visions of remaining the same size, of Molly, her cat, carrying them around carefully in her mouth protecting them from other cats because … they were the size of a mouse.

"Naldo and I would have a tough time cleaning rooms or serving pancakes if we remained this size. In fact, I think it would be frowned upon by the cruise staff if we could be mistaken for cockroaches?" Joel, always the joker, attempted to joke. It failed to cheer anyone up.

This was serious. Grace sunk deeper into the white sofa. She suddenly felt homesick for her parents, cat and friends.

Pixel interrupted Grace's thoughts, speaking sadly. "I'm just so worried about Stryker and the Pearlball teams. Professor Elk mentioned he thought the Weavers were heading towards the arena. I am sure they won't wait. They are probably there now. The teams are in danger. Stryker is in danger."

It was true. Stryker and the Pearlball Team had a lot to worry about too; at least on the white sofa they were safe for now.

Sam shifted nervously in his seat by Grace. He was worried. So he did what he always did if he was sad, nervous or confused (but equally when he was happy, excited or bored), he switched on his Magigad and started to fiddle through the many features. The distractions of all the options on the Magigad, he found calming. Grace never understood this and found it rather frustrating, she would much rather talk about it out loud.

"Oh my goodness," Pixel whose voice had been calm now almost screamed, but even then somehow her raised voice sounded melodic. "What are we going to do? We have to think up a plan. We can't stay here forever. We have to save her. "

Geeko was pacing up and down in front of the white sofa, a frown on his forehead deep in thought. "Pixel, we don't know how to get there. Plus, it's almost impossible to get out of here. We have been warned." He observed pointing at the sign and the troll guarding the door.

Joel and Naldo were sitting rather resignedly, sunk into the white chairs surrounded by white cushions. Naldo was munching noisily on the peanuts from the end table. His comfort method in a crisis must be to eat.

Pixel, however, was not eating. Or sitting. She was fluttering, noisily around above them. There was no logic to her flying; she flapped around like a fly who had exhausted itself on the inside of a window trying to get outside. Shoulders hunched, arms limp by her side but then her wings flapping like crazy. Up a little, down a little, left, right, repeat. She was muttering "Stryker's in danger," over and over again in a quiet voice. It was both disturbing but strangely mesmerizing to watch, like a beautiful, if not very erratic dance. Naldo, Joel and Geeko paid no attention. They had obviously witnessed this behavior before.

"I've got it," shouted Sam. Though he was probably the last one in the group Grace thought would break the silence, he did.

He lowered his voice, "The Magigad has picked up the location of the Pearlball Tournament. It seems to have hacked into the Trackle information before it was wiped. The Magigad Nerd Wizard Code Breaking Mode was left on. The elf at the desk mustn't have had time to turn it off. That would certainly be a reason why her sensor went off. The Magigad Nerd Wizard Code Breaking Mode would definitely be in violation and something an 'Honesty Scan' or 'Pureness test' would and should pick up.

It's fantastic though, I have only ever used it to spy in on Grace texting her friends on the old iPad Mom gave her. It's awesome. All the information is still here. We have to get out of here, find our way to the Pearlball Tournament, track down the lost Trackle, return it, save Stryker and the Magical Kingdom and return to the Boredom victorious! I mean the Brilldom."

Joel, Naldo and Geeko all crowded around Sam behind him so they could see the Magigad screen."Let me see!" Geeko said excitedly. Even Pixel stopped her frenzied dance and flew down to land on the seat beside Sam.

Grace decided to ignore the fact Sam had been hacking into her texting conversations; at least for now. She joined the rest of the gang to see the Magigad screen. The whole plan seemed a little far-fetched to her. How could they save anyone? But what other choice did she have- she stared at the screen.

Chapter 15

The Prototype Portal

There was a buzz of excitement between the friends, as they all saw the information the Magigad had picked up and retained.

"Excellent," said Joel admiringly, "The Magigad Nerd Wizard Code has picked up all the information from the Trackle. That is amazing. It is lucky that the Weavers didn't know they could have just bought a Magigad 3000. Imagine if they had found out it was that easy. The Magical Coalition will have to know about the flaw though. They will be pretty mad about that." He looked at Geeko presuming he would agree.

But Geeko was not listening. He was concentrating on something else. His broad forehead wrinkled into a frown underneath his cap. All of a sudden a big smile came across Geeko's face and his frown ceased to exist

"I have just the way to escape; we shouldn't tell the Magical Coalition yet," He had been listening after all. "They are way too busy making everyone safe. We can use the Magigad. We can use it to get to the Pearlball Tournament. Then we will work out a plan to get back the stolen Trackle. Let the adventure begin ... girls, you stay here."

"No way!!" said Pixel and Grace in unison. "If you are going, we are all going!!"

Geeko grinned to Sam, Joel and Naldo, "I knew I would not get away with that! You just cannot be a gentleman in this day and age.

Come this way. I think I have worked out how we can get out without alarming the trolls. They have enough to do."

The group pushed through the crowds and out into a hallway, past the restrooms and around a corner to a small door marked with a bright red sign saying 'Staff only'.

Geeko did a quick look left and right and noticed that no one was watching them in the chaos, and that all the security staff had been redirected to other areas. Geeko confidently pushed open the door, which led to a small cupboard full of cleaning supplies. He switched on the light. The group squished in between futuristic looking vacuum cleaners, buckets and various plastic bottles labeled with interesting names such as 'Sparkle-Bright' "Whiter than White" and "Pixiedust Remover."

Looking around from her view between Naldo's elbow and Pixel's wing pocket, Grace began to wonder if all her adventures were going to involve a cupboard of some kind or another and maybe cleaning products; be that dust products or laundry detergent.

Geeko closed the door, strategically moved some of the bottles and a vacuum to the side, then took a credit card-like object from his pocket. The card was attached to his pocket by a long elastic cord. He motioned for the group to stand together and asked Pixel politely to please stop flying around and stand for a minute. Then he pushed the card like a hotel keycard into a slot hidden under the light switch. Immediately, the floor fell from beneath their feet. It was not a long fall, (maybe only a few inches in real measurement), but for a fairy sized person, it was the equivalent of a few feet and it surprised them all. It surprised them all, except for Geeko of course, who motioned to their left where the slight drop had left a gap from which a shaft of light shone.

"Time to crawl," He instructed. "Welcome to the Portal prototype number one. A little primitive compared to the other and no size changer for you human guys, but nevertheless not bad for a first attempt. We do have to put more effort into this version though."

They all crawled into the narrow gap and inched towards the shaft of light in front. Geeko followed behind, pulling sharply at the elastic cord attached to the card which was still in the light switch. With perfect precision the cord retracted bringing the card safely back to Geeko before the floor shot back up to its original location revealing a wall of stone behind it.

"I told you it was primitive," Geeko observed, "Crawl on crewmates!" For about four minutes, the friends half scooted, half crawled toward the light. Grace did not want to be the first to complain, but the gap was rather awkward. The ground was uneven making it too uncomfortable to crawl on but it was not a high enough gap to walk in, which made the only option a half squat half crouch. Grace felt like an elderly penguin with arthritis. She could hear some giggling from behind her which made her think she also looked like an arthritic penguin. She looked ahead at Sam and Joel. She had to admit, if she looked anything like them, it was a funny sight.

Pixel was the only one who looked vaguely comfortable. Firstly, she was slightly smaller than the others and secondly, she had activated her wings and was hovering horizontally; her hands in front of her like a winged superman. She may have been more comfortable, but as there was only just enough room for her body and wings to fit, she needed to concentrate hard not to squash her wings on the ceiling or bang her nose on the uneven ground. Grace was sure Pixel was worried about her beautiful wing chitin.

One by one, they slid out of the shaft into a bigger area instinctively stretching out the rather cramped parts of their bodies. Naldo broke the silence rubbing his back.

"Good grief Geeko! Could you not have made that shaft a couple of inches higher?"

"Everyone's a critic," Geeko replied good naturedly. " You have to remember I was only a young gnome when I made this and I fitted perfectly. Plus, there is a reason it is called a prototype. That is unless they have changed the definition of prototype recently. It is a first attempt; practice not perfection, my friends. The first prototypes are rarely perfection. In science, mistakes are just ways to push you in the right direction. Error is your most useful assistant if you are only brave enough to listen. Losers quit when they fail. Winners fail until they succeed ... Oh and Naldo a little yoga on your agenda would not go amiss? Just saying!!"

Naldo smiled sheepishly. Geeko moved over to a part of the wall where a strange contraption was attached, which looked like a vertical conveyor belt.

"I never did decide on a good name for this method of getting us above ground," Geeko confessed. "I used a reclaimed, recycled, baggage claim conveyor belt from the port. You know the ones; used to take the cruise passenger's luggage to and from the ship to the arrival or departure lounge. I added some little ledges." he pointed to a rather narrow ledge a little bit wider than a ladder rung. The rungs were placed at regular intervals on the belt. As Sam followed the rungs up with his eyes, he saw that instead of going round and round as it had done with luggage, this conveyor belt went up through the ceiling and into a whole heading upwards.

Geeko, still talking, moved over to a switch to the side of the conveyor belt. He pushed it and the belt began to move, taking the rungs up through the tube. The rungs kept moving upwards then presumably at the top they came back down via the belt. It was like an escalator belt Sam had once seen being repaired at the underground, only much steeper and not as safe looking.

"I thought about naming it 'The Folk Flinger' or the 'Rung Rocket' but nothing seemed quite right ... Okay, who is first?" Geeko said, knocking an enormous spiderweb off the entry to the silver tube. As he did, the moving conveyor belt brought around an enormous spider. So big it had to squash itself into the silver tube. It saw Geeko with the bits of its perfectly made web still hanging from his hand. The spider's eyes flashed furiously at Geeko and the group. The spider was certainly less than impressed about the situation. It had no doubt had the shaft to itself for a good while. It did not like its web being disturbed. Judging by the fierce look on its face, it was also probably not registered on the Animal Kingdom Trackle app. It looked rather like it might want to eat them for lunch rather than help them.

Pixel screamed. Grace rushed backwards so fast she nearly knocked Naldo and Joel over like giant dominoes. The spider attempted to dismount the rung it was balanced on into their room. Geeko casually pushed the lever which had started the belt and made the rungs go around faster. The spider stumbled on it's dismount making one of its legs tangle around the other so instead of dismounting into the room it shot back up through the tube in the ceiling.

"Sorry, didn't realize that you were still using that," Geeko shouted up the chute to the spider "I guess I haven't used this chute for a while! It has a new resident."

He turned to the startled group, who were now standing much closer to each other in anticipation of the spider returning around the belt.

"Opps," observed Geeko directing his attention to the cowering group. "That spider did not look happy. Let us head on up before he comes back down the other side and untangles itself. Sam, you go first" He gently pushed Sam towards the belt. "Jump on. You have to be fast." He then pushed Sam a little more aggressively.

Sam shot towards the conveyor belt, stumbled his feet onto a rung, grabbed the rung higher up with his hands and was forced full throttle upwards. The silver tube enclosed around him giving the illusion he was going much faster than he was.

Below, he heard various shrieks and scrambling as the others piled onto the rungs either encouraged or pushed by Geeko, or were just eager to escape the room before the huge spider returned around the belt. There would be no way out of the room if the spider returned as the narrow entrance had closed behind them.

Sam knew everyone was safely aboard when he heard the echoing voice of Geeko shout "Whee, I had forgotten how much fun this was. Sam. I forgot to tell you. When you see the light shine behind you, jump backwards into the room. Otherwise you will flip back around the end of the belt and back down the other side. Trust me it is no fun going down upside down. Everyone else, follow Sam's lead."

Sam was beginning to panic a little. Being first was not always fun. Not only was he the one with the responsibility of finding the light and jumping backwards and he would have to mentor the others to find the same route. Plus, every now and then he was covered by huge cobwebs making it hard to see. That spider was not going to be happy with them if it ever caught them up.

Sam pushed the cobwebs aside and looked up. He could see a gap in the hole further along through which a light shone down. Sam braced himself to jump backwards. He counted slowly in his head trying to time his jump to perfection: 10, 9 ,8, 7, 6, 5, 4, 3, 2, 1 ... jump !

Chapter 16

Seedsurfing

Sam lay on his back panting: both the tension and landing had taken his breath away. Luckily, the landing was pretty soft. He scrambled to his feet and rushed over to the gap through which he could see the empty rungs on the conveyor belt flying by. He gingerly peered down the silver tube ready to help the others. He could see the top of Naldo's head coming up towards him. "Jump," shouted Sam and Naldo plummeted backwards into the room and onto the soft landing which looked like a pile of huge tarp bags.

Joel, coached by Sam, jumped back safely too, followed by Pixel who jumped backwards then fluttered gracefully, not even hitting the ground. She gently landed next to the boys and began to brush the cobwebs off her wings.

Grace's arrival was not as graceful, despite Sam's expertly timed shout to jump. Grace did not jump backwards and it was only because Sam grabbed the back of her T-shirt and yanked her down into the room that she did not disappear further up the tube and round the bend to descend the other side.

The whole event reminded Sam of the first time he and Grace had ski lessons. They had taken the chairlift back up to the top of the mountain. The skichair was just about to reach the top and the passengers in front were exiting when Sam realized Grace was not moving to exit. Grace had told him later that her ski goggles had steamed up so she couldn't see and she had her ski hat and earmuffs on so tight that she couldn't hear. Sam at the last minute had to push Grace off, then scoot himself off and to the side before the ski chair went around the big wheel and descended back down the mountain.

The result of his heroic rescue was that he tripped over his skis and ended up on top of Grace in a pile of snow which the ski chair attendants had neatly piled to the left of the exit. Their sticks and skis were all tangled up. Oh, and of course the cute girl in their ski class had been in the ski chair behind them and seen all the drama which to her looked as though Sam had just tripped and pushed his sister into the snow. She made a graceful exit and skied elegantly towards the rest of the group. The group of course happened to be conveniently positioned perfectly to get a wonderful view of Grace and Sam's long winded untangling of skis and ski poles. Grace was not thrilled about her rescue.

At least this time Grace was a little more thankful. "Thanks," she whispered breathlessly from the pile of tarp bags.

Geeko needed no such help. He jumped back landing on his feet as though he had done it a thousand times. And maybe he had.

"Good Grace rescue Sam," Geeko commented on having watched Sam's rescue of Grace from below. He slid a door closed blocking the entrance to the hole. Grace was sure that she glimpsed a big hairy spider's foot fly by as the door swung closed. She hoped that they did not have to return this way.

"Silver Bullet," said Joel. The others looked at him confused.

"The Prototype should be named the Silver Bullet."

Geeko smiled "Great name Joel. The Silver Bullet it is. Now let's look at the Magigad and get to the Tournament as fast as we can." Grace thought "*Huge Spider's House' or Don't Go In' would be better names, even the original People Flinger.*"

Sam took out his Magigad and they all huddled around the screen while Geeko pointed out where they were: a storage area of the port for the tarp covers they put on top of baggage carts when it rains. The rooms and the tarps of course seemed huge because of their relative size.

"We need to get from here," Geeko pointed, indicating where they were, "to here." He motioned to part of the map with a drawing of an oyster shell on it. It seemed a long way. Sam began to wonder how they could possibly get there, especially considering their relative size to the scale of the map.

Grace vocalized his concern, "How on earth will we get there? "

"The old fashioned way," said Geeko. "Pixel won't have any problem flying, but everyone else can't cover the ground as fast as we need to. It might take a little practice but I know you can do it."

The group followed Geeko outside. Outside, everything was very disorientating as they were so small. They were obviously on a gravel path of some kind. But instead of the gravel making it easier to walk on, as it would have if they were their normal size, it made it much harder to navigate.

They stumbled over each piece of grit as though it was a huge boulder. Pixel of course glided with ease over them, her pretty wings fluttering gently. Occasionally, Pixel would lean down and steady Sam or Grace as they stumbled over the uneven ground. Finally, they arrived at the grassy area and the terrain changed from boulder-like stones to a forest of grass, each blade towering above them like bamboo shoots. Pixel landed on the ground beside them. Walking covered the ground faster than flying in and out of the giant blades of grass.

Once fully inside the covering of grass, Geeko motioned to the group to stop and listen carefully. After a moment he looked relieved and said, "Good no lawn mowing today ... that would have been a disaster." Grace and Sam could see why this would have posed a problem. They did not want to be confronted by a giant lawnmower. Being small was so difficult.

They followed Geeko, who had picked up speed, and was now proceeding in a left and right zigzag, in and out of the huge blades of grass, his eyes peering upwards at the sky. The children wondered what he was looking for, but it did not take long for him to explain.

"Seedsurfing is our only option. The wind direction and the time of year are perfect."

Grace wondered what 'Seedsurfing' was and why the time of year and wind direction were important. Once again, she did not have to wait long until the answers were revealed.

"The seeds are perfect in the summer, this would be so much harder in the winter," Geeko pointed up at the shoot they were standing right next to. To Grace and Sam, it resembled a huge green fireman's pole surrounded by broad deep green leaves. Right at the top was a familiar looking yet huge seed, it just had to be a dandelion. The summer had made its deep yellow color change to seeds making the flower have a circle of seeds or spores, which looked like huge silver umbrellas blown inside out.

"Excellent!!" Joel interrupted as everyone else silently strained their necks upwards, "Seedsurfing ... sounds fun ... but how does that work again?" Sam could tell he was a little nervous and had obviously never done seedsurfing before.

Geeko smiled "You are going to love this. You have all seen Mary Poppins right? She dances in the air with her umbrella above her head? Well, same theory for seedsurfing. You simply grab a seed pod at the base, pull it out, run off the flower and jump. The wind will do the rest. Pixel you can help out if anyone seems to be going off course. Either give them a gentle push or flutter your own wings underneath really fast causing a draft wafting them the right direction."

Naldo saw a flaw in the plan, "Ermm and how do we come down? Do we jump"

Grace hoped not, she had had enough of rough landings and bruising herself for one day.

"Oh, it's easy," answered Geeko with an air of confidence. "Each seed pod is made up of a clump of seeds. You simply reach up and pull a seed off the pod, one at a time. The art of it is not to pull too many off at the same time. You can make a very graceful descent. When my dad went to school there were classes on seed surfing and seed surfing competitions. My dad got to the final of The Gnome Interscholastic Seedsurfing Tournament. Points were given for the faster you went up, then the closer you got to the target landing spot. Bonus marks for style of course. They didn't offer it in my school, Trackles have almost made the sport obsolete. Most folk just summon a friendly animal to help them. My dad and I spent many a Sunday afternoon gliding around the park. Those were the days, now even my ad prefers the Animal Kingdom Trackle App." concluded Geeko chuckling.

Pixel filled the kids in on the details. "You use the Animal Kingdom Trackle App to find magical animals or magical folk to transport you where you want to go. Birds, owls, butterflies, beetles, rabbits, even the odd squirrel or cat will help, if they are registered. Professor Elk said they were going to help with search and rescue today. The creatures need to be registered though. It used to be that the animal and insect community were all friends of the magical world. But sadly that is not true any more. Some of them have lost their magical abilities and some have become mean to us. There is research from the magical confederation to show that all the pesticides which humans use on crops and leak into the water supplies, together with other bad human influences have stunted a lot of their compatibility with the magical world. It is a shame. You just don't know without the using the app if an animal is going to help you out or eat you."

Geeko sighed sadly "One of magical folks traditionally best friends, the swallows have been particularly hard hit, they used to be a reliable form of companionship and means of travel, but now you have to watch out that they don't swoop down and feed you to their fledglings. Beautiful creatures, but they seem to have turned on us."

"The owl however is still pretty reliable. Their magical ties are simply too strong and they have a deep intelligence, which enables them to find food unaffected by human chemicals. They are also nocturnal and have little contact with humans. Swallows, however, often live under the eaves of human houses. So they have no ability to keep away from the chemicals that humans use on the fields or in their homes. It is sad. Humans have no idea how hard they make it for us or what effects their pesticides and cleaning products have on nature. I am just so glad the Magical Kingdom is so adaptable"

Sam felt very guilty about the human's influence over the Magical Kingdom but he was very glad about the owls. Owls were his favorite.

"So, how are we going to know when to come down? And how do we do that again?" asked Naldo, skillfully changing the subject from the bad behavior of humans. He was obviously also uncomfortable with the conversation.

"I would suggest that when you see the row of pearl shells sticking out of the ground, start plucking off the seeds," advised Geeko. "That should work. We will aim to meet to the right of the goal posts. Pixel will keep us all in line. Right Pixel?"

"We've got this Geeko. I have looked at the directions on Sam's Magigad and am ready to assist," Pixel confirmed, saluting.

Chapter 17

Torments and Terror

Climbing up the stem of the flower seemed like a hard prospect, but it was not as hard as Grace first thought. Each stem had little groves on it which could be used as foot and hand holders similar to rock climbing grips. Grace wondered if you could see them at all when you were normal size. She vowed to look when she got back to her real size, if she ever got back to her real size. She sighed to herself.

They cautiously made their way up. Sam laughed, thinking they must look like multicolored ladybugs, climbing up the flower's stem all in a row. He stopped laughing when the world went dark for a second. He looked up and saw that the darkness was caused by the shadow of a bird way up high above them. He studied it for a moment. Was it a swallow? He shuddered at the thought of Geeko's earlier talk about some birds wanting to eat the magical folk. Surely he was imagining it. There are thousands of varieties of birds. But also he thought if they did look like exotic ladybugs they would look like a delicious treat to any bird. He climbed a little faster passing Joel.

Sam reached the top and was surprised to find a hole up to the flowerhead from the stem. No need to do any skilful mountaineering moves up and over the top. "Genius, this nature thing" thought Sam. He stuck his head out and found Pixel, who had flown up and was waiting patiently leaning on a seed.

Geeko, Grace, Joel and Reynaldo were close behind and soon poked their heads up from the hole.

On examination of the seeds, it was obvious that the flower they had climbed was indeed a dandelion. The seeds above them opened up like big silver umbrellas just as Geeko had suggested.

"The silver seeds are called 'florets'; together with the stem they are called pods" explained Pixel casually "and they are just perfect." She touched the stem of the floret behind her gently and the silver umbrella rocked gently. "This late in the summer, they are almost ready to be blown off by the wind themselves. We won't have to yank them out either. They will come straight out. I hate when you see folks yanking them before they are ready to fly. The seeds are discarded at the end of the journey and don't make quite as strong flowers as they would if they were allowed to get to full maturity," she made a little sigh and stroked the pod again and the silver floret swayed slowly.

"Her grandma was a flower fairy," explained Reynaldo quietly leaning in closer to Grace and Sam so Pixel couldn't hear. "So flower protection is in her blood... don't start her off about endangered flowers. When the cruise ship took us to Gibraltar, she had us climb up the Rock on a goat to see if we could find the rare flower, the Gibraltar Champion Selena. Man, that was a rough day ... the track was really narrow and slippy and goats really smell when it rains. I went back to the ship smelling like a cross between a wet dog and moldy goat's cheese," he added grinning.

"Don't think I can't hear you Reynaldo." snapped Pixel giving Naldo a glare "Fairies have over average hearing. It was the Gibraltar *Campion Silene Tomentosa*, actually, so get your facts right Naldo and the goat was very nice to take us all that way in the rain."

"Oh sorry Pixel." replied Naldo "I forgot about the 'tormentosa' part of the flower. Finding it was certainly a 'torment for us-a'."

Joel laughed loudly at Naldo's play on words, getting in on the joke. "Torment-us-er," he repeated, still laughing "You should have been there. The goat was grumpy and Naldo was right, very wet and smelly. The goat refused to take directions and ended up on the other side of the Rock to where we wanted to be. When we tried to correct him, he bucked us all off and almost peed on Geeko. Eventually he ditched us. Luckily, we found a friendly deer to take us round to the right side."

"So, finally, we find the 'Torment-us flower'. It was all droopy from the rain and we had to stop the deer from eating it. Pixel was a little over enthusiastic about taking her selfie with it about a hundred times. So, we were left trying to keep the hungry deer away from his favored lunch. Apparently as it is so rare, it is also a delicacy for deer. In the end the deer got hungry and so fed up with us telling it what it could and couldn't eat, that it bounded off merrily without waiting for us."

Naldo continued, "We couldn't get any response from the Animal Kingdom app because we were so high up. So, we ended up having to jog down the Rock. We only just made it back in time to catch the cruise ship before it pulled out of port. No time for a shower. I have never been so wet. Or smelly. The cruise chef was so cross with me, he made me shower, then mop the entire kitchen twice after my shift."

"Enough talking," said Pixel. "Oh and if you want me to help guide you to the Pearlball Pitch, I would watch your words. I had a lovely day with the *Campion Silene Tomentosa*. It was well worth the trip."

"Only because she could fly down the mountain and had packed an umbrella." grumbled, Naldo.

"Let's pick a pod," suggested Geeko, tactfully changing the subject. "Look for long stems and lots of seeds," Geeko picked one out, gently teasing it free from the flower at the bottom. "You are right, Pixel. The pods are perfect, one little waggle and they come free. A couple more weeks and we would have a job finding a dandelion with seeds left. We would have to choose Milkweed. They are not quite as easy to navigate. And winter is impossible for seed surfing, you can't find the right plant to save your life."

By the time Geeko had finished talking, Naldo, Joel and Sam had chosen their pods. Grace, considering a few options, eventually had found the perfect one and gently plucked it out. They were remarkably light and fragile. She wondered how they were going to carry them any distance at all.

Sam, Pixel and Geeko hunched over the Magigad one more time analyzing the Navigation screen, which showed them the distance between them and the Pearlball Pitch. Geeko made some mental calculations including the old trick of putting up your finger to see which direction the wind was blowing.

"Okay, we need to all bend the bottom of our pods to make a footstep to hang on to," he expertly twisted the bottom of his pod upwards. Then he proceeded to help Grace and Sam. "According to my calculations, we need to jump this way." decided Geeko. "I'll go first, follow me. Just hold on to the pod. Run in the same direction as I do and jump. Pixel will push us if we get off course."

He held his pod in both hands in front of him and ran towards the edge of the flower head and just before the end, the wind blew under the seeds of his pod and lifted him up gently. He gracefully hopped onto the footrest nature had made, then turned and grinned, motioning to the others to follow. Pixel hovered above waiting for them all to mount their pods.

Naldo went next, followed by Joel whose pod flew off so fast that he had to scramble to reach his foothold. When he reached it he shouted "Excellent," and made a motion like a cowboy with a lasso. "I am riding the seed, dudes. Yeehaw."

Grace took advantage of the surge of confidence she felt from seeing Joel so happy; she took a deep breath and ran full pelt to the end of the flower head, her hands firmly placed around the pod. Gently, the pod rose upwards. Grace found it surprisingly easy to step onto the footrest. She rose with the others above the field. Her hair blew in the wind and she relaxed. This was fun.

Sam was right behind her. He ran, jumped and hoisted himself onto the footrest. "This is easy," he thought to himself. Pixel brought up the rear flying back and forth between the pods. After a while she flew to the front in anticipation that the Pearlball Pitch might come into view at any time and she could be ready to assist with the descent.

Sam's pod was not as fast as the others. He had chosen a pod with less developed seeds. But he was moving along. He was just wondering if he could get out his Magigad and listen to some tunes when the sky went dark. A big shadow cast above him.

"Oh no," thought Sam. "A bird?"

He looked up nervously hoping he was mistaken, but there it was. The bird looked like a huge jet plane, wings outstretched gliding effortlessly above him. Sam noted the 'V' shaped tail and wings silhouetted in the sun. Classic shape of a swallow, Sam noted miserably. He remembered back to a third grade project in science when they had to record and identify the birds visiting their yard for a week. When they had compiled the bar chart, he had the most swallows in his yard. He remembered admiring their ability to catch flies mid-flight zigzagging through the sky and scooping up mosquitos. Now, Sam feared that he too might become a mid-flight snack. Sam moved himself in closer to the pod's stem. Maybe it wouldn't notice him. But it was too late.

The bird took a dive towards him. Sam could see his silver beak gleaming in the sunlight. The dark shadow streamlined its body towards the pod below.

Sam had to think fast.

He fumbled in his pocket almost losing his hold. His pod launched upwards suddenly. The swallow plucked the pod and Sam out of the sky. Sam was spun and jerked around rapidly. He was quickly losing his grip on the pod and his foothold was bouncing up and down making it hard to stand on. Sam was pulled sharply sideways. There were only seconds to act before he fell below into the green grass which seemed so far below. Then there it was ... a loud siren sounded from his pocket. He had managed to reach in his pocket and activate the panic alarm on the Magigad. The swallow with its ultra sensitive hearing panicked, dropped the pod and whizzed off into the distance.

The pod abruptly dropped, twisted and twirled even more disorienting Sam. Eventually, returning to a slow calm motion. Sam assessed the situation. His pod had lost a few seeds and its shape where the swallow had held it in its beak, but at least it was still flying. Sam was just not certain if it was in the right direction.

Chapter 18

A Soft Landing

Sam managed to turn the ear breaking Magigad alarm off. He was scared that the swallow might return, but the noise was hurting his ears. Feeling dizzy and with the alarm sound still ringing in his ears, he looked around. He could not see the others. The swallow must have taken him further away than he thought.

It was eerily quiet up there on his own and he realized he was dropping down slowly. Probably because of the seeds he had lost.

He began to plan. When he landed he could look on the Magigad for the Pearlball pitch and make his way there but depending where he was, it could take a very long time. Maybe he should start pulling seeds and land now in case he was traveling further away. He had just decided this was the best idea when he heard a familiar voice.

"Phew. Sam are you okay?"

It was Pixel. Sam was so relieved that he almost lost his balance. He accidentally pulled out a seed as he rebalanced himself.

"Woah," Pixel gasped breathlessly. "We are going to need all those seeds to get you back on track. I really had to use my sprint wings to catch up to you. I also need to catch my breath."

She hovered floating for a while, hands on her hips, breathing hard. Gradually, her breathing recovered, but not before Sam had lost more ground.

"I'm ready now," she declared and got to work. She swooped under Sam and fluttered her wings making a breeze which lifted the pod back up. She then moved a little to the right and redirected him in the direction she had come from. Sam tried to stay still in order to make the process easier for Pixel.

After what seemed like a long time, Sam saw four tall shapes towering over the grass below. "Oyster shells on a pole. That must be the Pearlball pitch." Sam thought.

"Start pulling off the seeds," Pixel directed.

Sam started pulling as fast as he could. Unfortunately, he started pulling from just one side, the side the swallow had disturbed which made his pod even more lopsided, causing him to descend fast despite Pixel's help and also causing his pod to start to spin again.

"Pull slower and from the other side," Pixel yelled, trying desperately to correct Sam's imbalance by fluttering her wings faster. Seeing this was not working, she flew closer to try to grab the seeds from the other side and pluck them herself. Sam, who had not seen Pixel, was trying hard to follow directions, he balanced carefully on his tilted foothold and leaned over to grab more seeds.

The result of the combination of Pixel and Sam grabbing the same seed at the same time, (Pixel from above, Sam from below) was disastrous. It created just enough imbalance for Sam to lose his footing and dangle dangerously by one hand. To retain his balance, he grabbed a handful of seeds, which of course pulled straight out, causing him to descend super fast and made his dandelion floret spin around, making him dizzier and more disorientated. He closed his eyes and held on tightly with his left hand, as he struggled to keep hold. Just how long could he hold on and what would happen when he hit the ground at this speed?

He felt himself stop spinning and land abruptly but more gently than he expected. He seemed to have landed on what felt like a feathered bed. Still hanging tightly to what was left of the dandelion, he lay on his back, his eyes closed, relieved that he was not spinning and waiting for the dizziness to pass. As his world stopped spinning, he opened his eyes and saw the clear blue sky above. For a split second he wondered if it was all a dream and he was in fact back at home and had somehow dozed off in his backyard. Then he heard a familiar voice.

"Hey Sam, great soft landing I found you right?" He sat up and saw Pixel sat beside him cross legged, her wings folded behind her. "But dude, I am never supervising your Seedsurfing again. You are one crazy surfer dude. I resign as your seedsurfing supervisor... forever. "

Sam thought that was a little unfair seeing as he had just escaped from a hungry swallow but, nevertheless she had definitely saved him from a hard fall. He looked around and tried to get his bearings.

"Where am I?" he questioned Pixel, feeling a little lightheaded. He was lying on a huge beige soft mattress. The surface was nice and cool and he wasn't sure he wanted to leave.

"Just a little walk from the pitch. Hopefully the others made it okay, I had to sprint back to you just as Grace was landing. Here, just slide down the side." Pixel promptly disappeared over the edge of the off white pillow-like surface they had landed on.

As Sam followed her and slid over the side, he dropped onto the grass. Looking back up from underneath he saw an intricate black fan like pattern. Pixel saw that he was examining the canopy above him.

"It is a lamellae. Very beautiful specimen of clitocybe. I would say edible to humans but more useful as a landing spot, meeting point and occasional house to visiting fairies. The transitory fairies of the Morel or Lepiota family love to use these." She walked around the stalk examining it closely, running her hand gently along the surface. "No resident fairies at the moment though the stalk doesn't have any ridges. Very smooth."

Sam was still confused. He was beginning to think that Magical Folk had their own language. "What is it " He questioned.

"Oh Sam, I just told you. Weren't you listening?" she sighed. "It is a clitocybe mushroom. The perfect landing spot for a totally out-of-control, completely crazy learner seed surfer," she teased. "The white patterns above your head are the mushroom lamella or some people call them gills. A papery hymenophore rib on the underside of most mushroom species. It disperses spores allowing the mushroom to spread for more fungal growth. Like seeds for plants."

Once again a little too much information. "*Basically*," he thought, "*he had just landed on a huge mushroom. No wonder it was soft.*"

They headed off on foot following the navigation of the Magigad, dodging the grass blades which lined the way as tall as bamboo shoots. It was slow going, but they were making progress.

Chapter 19

Pearlball Pitch Peril

Meanwhile, the others had all landed safely with very little drama.

Admittedly, Grace had panicked a little, as she saw Pixel fly off back the way they came, but she recovered fast and pulled off the seeds as instructed by Geeko earlier, lowering herself slowly downwards. She had been able to control the speed by pulling faster or slower. She observed Geeko, Naldo and Joel ahead and tried to steady herself at the level they were. The only tricky bit was at the end, when the only seeds left were ones she had to reach for right around the backside of the floret. She quickly realized, the more equal on each side, the easier it was to balance. Time passed with speed as she got closer to the ground, but she landed almost perfectly by the others behind the towering oyster goalposts.

"That was excellent," said Joel, smiling. Naldo, who had landed a little further onto the pitch, ran up to them smiling, still holding what remained of the dandelion floret. "Awesome. I hope all those seeds I dropped make healthy dandelions. I feel as though I pulled off a hundred of the things. I had to throw down fistfuls at the end. Pixel would be proud," Naldo laughed looking around. "Where is Pixel? Come to think of it, where is Sam? "

Everyone looked around them and scoured the sky for signs of the two lost friends.

"I saw Pixel heading back," said Grace quietly, worried about her brother. "I couldn't see Sam though."

Being the oldest was a tough job; you had to always worry about the youngest. Sam had certainly had her worried before; flying head first over fences on his bike, while attempting to perform high speed stunts. Snow tubing out of control into areas of the slope marked **DANGER**; but never in her wildest dreams had she imagined she would ever have to worry about him floating away on a dandelion. How would she explain that to Mom and Dad?

"I am sure Pixel has it under control, Grace." Geeko reassured her. "Let's wait here for a while. This is the place we said we would meet. I am sure they will turn up soon. You all wait here a sec and I will be back. I saw something as I landed. Joel come with me."

Geeko and Joel dodged back through the long grass away from the pitch.

Naldo entertained and distracted Grace with more stories of Geeko's Aunt Veronica's cookies

He ended by saying "I'm so hungry I could eat a whole plate of Aunt Veronica's cookies!!" Grace also was feeling hungry especially after all that talk of cinnamon raisins and chocolate chips. It hadn't been too long since they were eating from the buffet, but it felt like a week.

As if he had read their minds, Geeko and Joel returned, carrying what was easily identifiable as a huge raspberry, carefully between them.

"May as well have a snack while we are waiting," grinned Geeko. He pulled off a seed, five times as big as a normal raspberry and passed it to Grace.

It was delicious and very juicy. One little part of the raspberry was like eating a whole carton. Grace felt better already.

She was even happier though, when she saw Pixel and Sam walking through the long grass along the edge of the pitch towards them.

Pixel started talking even before she got in hearing range, "Yum Rubus idaeus, the European red raspberry. What a great idea I'm starving. I hate walking." She plopped down next to the group and helped herself to the bounty. "Flying with wings is so much more sensible than seed surfing."

Sam followed behind smiling. Happy to see them, but as he sat down, he suddenly stopped smiling.

"Are you okay Grace?" he said, concerned "you're bleeding." He took her hand and true enough, red droplets were dripping from her hand.

After what seemed like a lifetime to Sam, Joel giggled.

"Sam, it's raspberry pulp." Sure enough as he looked around and saw the leftover raspberry which matched the pulp on Grace it was obvious.

They all laughed.

Sam filled them in on his close call with the swallow. Pixel described in detail her rescue, while they finished the raspberry.

Then it was time to turn their attention to the Pearlball pitch and their true rescue mission.

Chapter 20

Concealed Company

The pitch which spread before them was huge, at least it seemed that way to Sam and Grace at their current height. The grass had been perfectly cut, not only on the white marked pitch, but all around it and the four sturdy looking bleachers. Beyond the outer line, stones were arranged for the spectators to sit.

The oystershell goals on either side appeared as big as satellite dishes but looked like shiny venus flytraps. There were three on each side of the pitch. All were raised onto posts of differing heights in a symmetrical pattern. The heights of the posts closer to them were mirrored by the ones on the other side. The shells were the most amazing sight, they were a shimmery gray color and cast a shadow over the long grass behind them. The shadows changed in size as the shells opened and closed.

The shadows reminded Grace of clouds hiding the sun on a breezy day. The timing of the opening and closing was random, sometimes faster than others. When the shells opened, you could see inside. The outside of the shells themselves were a wonderful shiny pearl color, but inside they were even more impressive, the inside had a stunning multicolored metallic glow. It reflected the sunshine like a multicolored mirror, into a rainbow colored rays, which in turn reflected colored stripes onto the perfectly manicured pitch below. As the shells took turns opening and closing, the rays changed like a Kaleidoscope. It was a truly beautiful sight.

Grace thought it was stunning. She wondered how it would look with colorful magical folk chasing around in the pitch. She hoped she would get to see a game at some point. As she imagined two teams moving over the kaleidoscopic grass, throwing a beautiful pearl to each other, moving towards the oyster shell goalposts, attempting to score into the colorful metallic shells before they closed.

Suddenly, something caught her eye toward the center of the pitch. There was a slight change in the pattern of colors as though part of the color coordination was lagging slightly. She squinted her eyes to get a better view. Yes, sure enough, a spec of changing color was darting around towards them, which was slightly but only slightly behind the color change in timing.

"Look," whispered Grace to the others, motioning towards the spec of color almost but not quite perfectly camouflaged against the colored streaks of light reflected from the Oyster shells. As the group watched, it took them a second or two to follow Grace's finger and find the discrepancy. The only indication of movement was during the switch between colors and only for a faint second. Grace was not sure if she should be scared. She had yet to see a Weaver, maybe it was one coming their way. The others did not seem scared though, so she watched anxiously as the blur of slightly odd movement gradually got closer, until it was close enough that she could tell the shape was a fairy. Her wings a haze as she made her way, like a chameleon, across the pitch.

"It is Stryker," said Pixel, grinning broadly at the sight of her friend "She always was the best at concealment.".

"Concealment is a technique the Pearlball players use to confuse their opponents. They train themselves to switch colors in the rays of light. It is never absolutely perfect but some players are definitely better than others. It looks as though Stryker has certainly mastered the skill." explained Geeko.

They started towards her moving towards the pitch to meet her, but Stryker motioned to stay back under the safety of the longer grass. It was not more than a few moments until Stryker and Pixel were reunited. They hugged each other. Stryker smiled at everyone, but she put her finger on her lips to indicate everyone should stay quiet and motioned for them to move deeper into the long grass surrounding the pitch.

Finally when Stryker thought they were far enough away. Stryker broke the silence.

"I escaped." she exclaimed " the Weavers are in the club house on the other side of the Pearlball pitch. They have the whole team hostage. They have been using the broadcast services of the press box, to communicate with the Enchanted Alliance."

Stryker continued. "The Weavers are demanding the entire contents of the tooth fairy compound in exchange for the stolen Trackle and the team. They believe they can use the magical powder the tooth fairies make to make a concoction which will keep humans from getting old. They believe they can make millions and millions of dollars. "

Pixel gasped.

"It is true; people would pay millions to look young," thought Sam. He had once lost his Mom in the grocery store and found her looking at the face lotions. He had been amazed how many there were and how expensive some of them were. He could buy a good bag full of games for one tub.

"That's terrible. How did you escape?" asked Joel.

"Funny you should ask," Stryker said grinning, obviously delighted to retell the tale. "The crazy, egotistical Weavers made themselves small using some crazy machine which one of them had found on the Brilldom. He said they had come across two parts of it in the laundry room trash a few years ago and thought they could put it together." It was Geeko's turn to gasp as Stryker continued. "It took them years to adapt it ... and well, in fact, they weren't as smart as they thought. When they used it for the first time earlier today it had worked and shrunk everything ... except one man's nose," she giggled. "The one who's nose didn't change was such a vain man. He has these big muscles and an awful, orange tan. His nose must have been big and ugly already as now it was really really big and ugly. His nose was so big that he had to hold it up with those huge biceps of his. Or he would topple over onto his conk," she paused to giggle again. Despite the seriousness of this hostage situation, the image of the vain muscle guy holding his nose up had them all smiling.

"Oh man," interrupted Geeko sheepishly. "That must have been another original prototype for the Portal. I remember it well, I really wanted to help Joel and Naldo have some fun with us, and had this idea to shrink them. I had been practicing with socks from stuffed clothes from the laundry, but I could not get that prototype to stop acting in a radical manner, sometimes it left things too big, sometimes it made things too small. I would get shirts with one button left huge but the rest shrunk or sweaters with one sleeve left huge when everything else was shrunk. I eventually got disheartened and decided to start again from scratch. I was so frustrated I broke it in half and threw it in the laundry trash. I knew I should have been more careful."

"You practiced on laundry?" questioned Joel. "I remember the big laundry scandal about two years ago. We had the chief of security down to make us report anything suspicious. The passengers were not happy when they lost their laundry or it was returned in odd shapes and sizes. In fact they were fuming and made the cruise line pay for them to buy some new clothes at the next port.

"Hey, you should have practiced on metal too," continued Joel. He was remembering when his keys were left large and he had to carry them around all day.

"Oh, I did," said Geeko wistfully, remembering the many hours in the laundry room using the pennies left in people's pant pockets.

137

"Back to the present day problem," reasoned Naldo. "Was this big nosed guy bald by any chance, with a bad smell of talcum powder?" asked Naldo.

"Yes," said Stryker " I wondered what the smell was. But you are right - a mixture of talcum powder, sweat and bad aftershave," she looked surprised. "Do you know him? "

Naldo and Joel looked at each other. "Ferdinand," they said together without hesitation. "The Pilates instructor on the Brilldom," explained Naldo. "We always suspected him of being a Weaver."

"Excellent, about his nose," giggled Joel "That dude is so vain. His Pilates studio even has mirrors on the roof, that's how vain he is."

"Nasty piece of work too," added Naldo. "How many Weavers are there?

"Three," answered Stryker. "Ferdinand. A huge guy with a beard and big eyebrows, smelt of meatballs ... "

"That has to be Claus the Chef," noted Naldo. "Are his eyebrows dark black and do they meet in the middle?" Narrowing his forehead so his thin eyebrows almost met in a frown.

"Yes. That sounds like him and the meatball smell would now have an explanation," confirmed Stryker. "The other was a lady. She was thin with wrinkles and bad teeth. She had a bad smell of old people's perfume. Oh and long nails that curved at the end and were painted a bad shade of purple ... mauveish yellowy. Yuck!!"

"Madame Cleaver. I noticed that strange nail color at breakfast," Naldo stated decisively. "The French teacher. Did she have a funny accent?" he asked.

"Oh no not at all. She sounded just like she was from New Jersey. We had a training session there last spring, it was definitely that accent." Stryker added.

"Oh, I knew she wasn't French." gloated Joel "Didn't I tell you so Naldo. First time I saw her, I said her accent was phony. Plus, remember when we docked the ship in France and all those French dancers came on. No one could find Madame Cleaver to introduce her. I knew it was because she was afraid of being told her accent was lousy! New Jersey though, that is too funny."

"So, how did you actually escape?" persisted Naldo

"Well, I seized on Ferdinand's insecurities. I told him I knew a herb which would reduce his nose in size. One which grows in the grass behind the stands. He believed me, so I led him out of the clubhouse through the lobby to the entrance of the pitch, under the reporters stand. Coach leaves keys on the right hand side of the door so they are not forgotten. The door locks immediately when you close it. Coach locked us out a few times before he decided on a secret key. Well, I took the keys, unlocked the door, turned around and pretended to look surprised. "He's escaping," I shouted. Ferdinand looked around towards the stairs where I was pointing and let go of his nose. The weight of his gigantic nose tipped him over and he fell onto the tile floor," she giggled at the memory of him almost tripping over his own nose as he tried to get up.

"I rushed out of the door while his attention was elsewhere. Blood was streaming out of his nose like a red waterfall. I slammed the door locked behind me and tucked the keys under my shirt. I concealed myself all the way across the pitch in case any of the others were watching. I saw you straight away. You were standing there like a huge advertisement that the rescue party had arrived. Bright clothes, loud mouths! Anyhow, I think all the noise and commotion Ferdinand made covered that up. Amazing timing, but, I had to get to you fast to avoid being seen, luckily it looks like you fooled everyone but me with your obvious lack of concealment skills."

She paused for a breath, "So now that we are together we have to get back over and save the others. Any plans from the Enchanted Alliance?"

"We are not exactly from the Enchanted Alliance. Not officially anyway," admitted Pixel. She explained about the announcement in the Enchanted Lodge. "The Magical World was in chaos. They were really busy. So we had to come ourselves," she concluded. "These are my friends: Grace, Sam, Reynaldo or Naldo as we call him, Joel and Geeko. We have come to help."

Chapter 21

The Magical Magigad

"Thanks for coming. I really appreciate it. Pixel, you are a great friend and it looks as though you brought some more great friends with you. But no plan from the Enchanted Alliance then?" Stryker said sadly. "Greatest Pearlball team of all time and no rescue plan."

"I am sure they are working on it. They are a little stretched right now with the breach," commiserated Pixel. "What happened to all the fans?"

"Well that is a great story," Stryker answered. "You know that our mascot is an owl, right?"

"Yep," answered Pixel faithfully, "Wootie."

"Wootie might have earned himself a medal. As soon as the Code One went out, he took it on himself to warn the fans. He flew to them and escorted them to the safe zone. Went back and forth until everyone was safe, then he stayed there to help guard the doors. He is a hero."

"Excellent," Commented Joel. "Now we need to find a plan that is as brave, to save the team ..."

"Aha," Geeko interrupted. "We do have a plan though. But we need your help, Stryker."

Geeko and Naldo were gathered around Sam and his Magigad. They made way for the others. Sam had zoomed the Magigad map into the small building across the field.

"Cool Sam," Stryker observed. "Your Magigad has drawn us a map of the inside of the clubhouse."

"Where are they holding the hostages?" asked Naldo.

Stryker pointed and Sam zoomed in the screen even closer and looked at the map.

"Wow, this is cool Sam. That is exactly what the clubhouse building looks like. Downstairs are the doors out to the pitch; that is where I came out with the Weaver guy, Ferdinand. If we ever go that way, be careful there may be blood on the ground from his nosebleed. Ughh" Stryker pointed straight across the field to the building behind the far side oystershell goals. "On the ground floor at the back on the left and right, are the changing rooms and in the middle stairs up to the commentary room, cafeteria and gym. The commentary room is really posh. It has really plush red carpets and comfy sofas. Occasionally we get to go up there for interviews."

Sam labeled the rooms on the screen as she spoke.

"There is a big glass window at the front so the press can see the game and the TV reporters can record straight through. The commentators and reporters have a glass soundproof box right in the middle. It is kind of a really cool glass deck. The cleaner has a job keeping it all clean, keeping fingerprints off all those windows. For this reason the commentary box is usually out of bounds until the game starts, so no one can mess it up with their fingers. We call it the Glass Box, even the floor is made with reinforced glass."

"Luckily, none of the reporters or commentators had arrived yet, they had been delayed at the last event in Greece. Our opponents hadn't made it out of the Muffle yet they had some hawks reserved to get them here fast. So it is just our team in there."

"What did you say his name was? The orange skinned weaver with the big nose? Ferdinand? Well he took a liking to the upstairs commentary box so we were all taken up there. We had to sit on the floor while they sat on the comfy white sofas and the weaver lady used the intercom to contact the Enchanted Alliance," finished Stryker.

"Can you contact any of your teammates?" asked Geeko.

"Hmmm, no. The Weavers made us give all our phones and electronics with them." Stryker paused. "... actually I might be able to, if we can get to Coach's locker. We put in ear microphones during practice so Coach can talk to us. They are on our earrings," Stryker pulled back her blonde hair and pointed to her pink pearl earrings. "The Weavers wouldn't know about them so it's not like they would make the team take them off. They look just like earrings after all. We can speak to the coach through our necklaces," she pointed to her matching pearl necklace, which she had tucked into her t-shirt next to a chain with a key. "But the coach's stereo system has to be turned on for any of this to work and it is not on. We can't speak to each other."

"Where is the stereo?" asked Sam.

"Where is the coach?" asked Grace.

Stryker answered both questions. "Coach has been taken hostage too. Coach is sitting on the floor with everyone else. The stereo is in his coach's office ... Do you really have a plan, Geeko?"

Geeko was looking very thoughtfully at the Magigad.

"Do you have the Spy App for the 3000?" he asked Sam. "I read about it in the Geomechanical Magic Magazine last year. There was a big controversy about the use of the electrophon in the Magical World and whether the electrophonic rays would pick up magical folk. One of the spy app features is that it can tell you from a distance where people are. It senses the heat and movement even through walls and buildings."

"Yes." interrupted Sam eagerly, "I got the app for Christmas. It is so cool. I used it on Grace and her friends when they were having a sleepover. They went to the movies four blocks from the house and it still could track them. The funniest bit though was back in the house, the girls were dancing around the room. The app tracked all their 'dance moves' . It was hilarious. I took a screenshot and sent it to our cousin Daniel. He thought I had edited it because they looked so silly."

"Hey, that's not fair," complained Grace. "Mom said you weren't to use it on people, only animals. No wonder Daniel cracked up when he asked if I had a fun time at my sleepover. You are so in trouble when I tell Mum." She turned to the others, "The app was a controversy in the human world too. It was nearly banned. It had been used to track all kinds of things causing so many complaints. Kids were tracking their parents' whereabouts, checking what their teachers did after school. Plus finding out their boyfriends were spending a lot of time with other girls, or vice versa, it was terrible. I am not surprised Magical Folk were worried. The humans were too."

Sam looked to Grace as though he still might think it was more fun than she did.

Sam continued, he obviously knew a lot about the app, "The company which coded the app got taken to court. They were forced to do an update, now you cannot see who the person is; it just looks like shadows and they mostly look the same. It was supposed to make people anonymous, so it was harder to track. It is still thought that the app may be totally recalled in the future. It was only a matter of days though before some clever kid worked out how to relabel people. He posted the hack on the internet so everyone can do it. The people look like the people on the Marauders Map from Harry Potter. Little shadows with their names above them. Once a name is on a shadow you can still track it. It's awesome. I really want to meet that dude."

Grace frowned. She had not forgiven him, that was the second time in an hour he had confessed to spying on her. Mom was not going to like this.

Pixel however was more concerned about the safety of Magical Folk.

"So ... Can it track Magical folk, Geeko? What did the article in the Geomechanical Magic Magazine say?"

"Well." explained Geeko. "The article said that the Enchanted Alliance had some concerns, so they ordered the Department of Magology to do a full report. They took apart a Magigad, Electrophon and all. They concluded that the Electrophon combined with the app could only pick up the size of humans. Fairies, gnomes and other magical folks are too small."

"Phew," said Pixel, relieved.

"I'm happy that the Magical Folk don't have to worry about being tracked by the humans on the Magigad. But part of the master plan was knowing where the weavers are by using the spy app," noted Geeko.

"It's been shrunk though," observed Grace putting her hostility to spying aside. "The Magigad has shrunk. Maybe it can locate things of our size now as it was programmed to find things of a relative size? We are smaller now and so is the Magigad. So are the Weavers."

"Clever idea," thought Sam, "only one way to find out if she was right."

He switched on the Magigad 3000's Electrophon and activated the spy app. "Fingers crossed."

"Fingers crossed," agreed Joel and Naldo in unison.

"I'm still not sure how the Magigad got shrunken?" mused Geeko. "I'll have to check that out at some point. Maybe the Airflush thought it was a watch. I did manage to work out a way to make jewelry and watches shrink. Or maybe ..."

Either way, the Magigad had shrunk and Grace was right; as the Magigad zoomed in to show the commentary box, they could see little shadows of people.

Sam began to hastily type. "So. Good news," he remarked. "It worked. I am labeling the two figures sitting on the sofa as 'Weaver 1' and 'Weaver 2' as we know that they are the only ones allowed on the sofas. I am labeling the shadow on the floor that is the biggest as the 'Coach'. Do you recognize anyone else Stryker ? So I can label them. That way we don't confuse the shadows."

Stryker giggled, "Coach isn't the biggest. I can tell that is Coach there." She pointed to the smallest shadow with a point on its head,"She is a Unicorn Pixie. " Stryker explained, "Very smart, fair and tough on conditioning exercises. Just like Unicorns but in Pixie size; clever, muscular and honest. The tallest is Chuckle. He is a gnome and the best goal scorer and a funny chap. So his name fits him just right. The shadow with the pigtails is Becca our fastest player. She makes up for Chuckle. Chuckle is strong and an accurate shot but not very fast, due to his height and the fact he is a gnome. No offense Geeko but gnomes are not the fastest of magical folk. Becca is fast so her role is to speed the ball up to him. Then he shoots."

One by one, Stryker identified each of the shadows and gave some great insider tips into the team. Camio, an elf, could be spotted as she was the smallest without the point Coach had. She had trained in Concealment since birth as her mother is an amphibian elf, closely studying chameleons. George, a tall but slender, friendly troll and the team's best catcher, was in charge of defending the goals along with his brother, Greg. Stryker found it hard to tell them apart by their shadows, but was pretty sure Greg had been wearing a hat. She said there would be no way of telling them apart had he not been wearing a hat. They looked like twins, Pixel observed, even though George was older. Grace felt relieved that she was not the only older sibling with a younger sibling just as tall.

Sam hastily typed and labeled each one. Until the shadows were complete with a name written above them. Stryker obviously knew her teammates well.

"Who is that?" asked Grace when there was only one person left to label.

"Hmm. I'm not sure," answered Stryker "Oh … I'm guessing it is Ms. Jessica, the elf cleaner. She must have turned up since I left.

Coach is really into cleanliness: another trait of a classic Unicorn pixie. She usually asks Ms. Jessica to come in after a game. But Ms Jessica is sweet, so she turns up before the game with homemade muffins. She likes to watch us play and she is very conscientious about the cleanliness of the clubhouse, especially the glasshouse. She likes to make sure everything is clean before, as well as after a game. Oh look there is her cleaning cart by the stairs. It is never far away from her in case she sees a spot that needs attention. She must be very worried about the white sofa. I bet some of Ferdinand's fake tan has rubbed off on it already. "

Chapter 22

The Plan

"One more thing we need to know is where the Trackles are being kept? Were they taken with the electronics? We will need to take them back to the Enchanted Alliance to make them all secure again so everyone can come out of the safe zones and use the Trackle system once more," requested Geeko.

"The ugly Weaver guy took all of them and tried to put them in a locker, but they wouldn't fit so he got frustrated and just locked them in the coach's office. I think they are just placed on the desk," Stryker answered.

"Funny thing is," she continued, "Coach is crazy about losing keys. I think I told you that is why she has multiple sets. One is left on a hook by the door to the pitch. Coach locked herself out so many times that Ms. Jessica suggested she have the same key for everything and make copies. Coach thought that was a great idea."

"Okay, that's great news," said Geeko. "Huddle around. Here is the plan. We need to get close enough to the clubhouse door, the one you came out of Stryker. We will gather there and check in with the Magigad that no shadows are close to the door; then we will use Coach's key to open it. Pixel, Stryker and I will go in. The rest of you will wait outside this window," he pointed to the Coach's office window. "Stryker and I will go to the stereo and start telling the team, by using their earring earphones, that they are about to be rescued. Pixel, you will get the Trackles and pass them through the window to Grace and Sam who will run and hide with them in the grass behind the home team bleachers."

He pointed to the tiered flat stone area behind the far end of the pitch. "Stryker, could you please give Pixel one of your earrings so you can stay in touch. Pixel, when you have finished passing the Trackles through you should exit via the window to go and meet the others at the bleachers."

Stryker and Pixel switched the clip on earring. Pixel joked about how unfashionable it was to be wearing an odd earring especially as she was about to rescue the most famous Pearlball team ever. Stryker laughed "We must remember to switch back before the press interview," she observed jokingly.

"I am sure the fans would be devastated to find out their hero wears mismatched earrings," Naldo continued in the voice of a TV reporter. "I can just hear it now: This is Magical world news. Today Trackles were stolen, the Magical World is in chaos, safe areas closed across the Magical Kingdom .....plus two fairies were seen today in mismatched earrings ... the world is in outrage."

They all giggled. Then, they got to work.

They used the long blades of grass surrounding the pitch to hide in. It was a longer route than across the pitch but, as they were not trained in concealment like Stryker, they did not want to risk being seen. After what seemed like a long hike, they were finally gathered at the side of the clubhouse ready to start 'the plan'.

Grace felt nervous. "*What if the plan didn't work? What if the Weavers took them hostage too? How would they ever get back to the ship before it left? What was the time anyway? It felt as though they had been away from the cruise a long time already. Were her parents back on board? What would happen if they missed the ship?*" She did not want to panic the others but the thought made her feel so nervous, she mentioned it to Sam.

"Sam, do you think we will miss the boat? What if Mum and Dad are looking for us?"

Sam looked blankly back at her. He had not thought about how much time was passing. He asked Naldo.

"Naldo, what time does the boat leave? Will we get back on time?"

Naldo looked at his watch, "I have it set on Magical Folk time. Magical Folk time is slightly slower than our time. Geeko once tried to explain why. Apparently, it is due to the moon rotation in relation to the size of your heart and proximity to earth's core. You know how Geeko explains things. It is totally confusing. I was lost after that. But you do notice if we see any humans, and by that I don't mean us or the Weavers as we are all preshrunk, the un-shrunken humans seem to be walking slightly slower than they really are. It is strange to see and to hear. When they talk it is so funny like deep slow motion voices. So we have about three slower hours until we have to return to the boat. About 30 minutes before the tour returns from the shore is crucial as that is when Joel and I have to get back to work. I will set my alarm for an hour before human time so we will know when to worry." Naldo fiddled with his watch. "There set. Now we don't have to worry till then."

Grace and Sam were totally confused about the strange timing, but were reassured as Naldo and Joel had done this a few times by now. The fact Naldo did not seem worried, at least not yet, reassured them.

"Okay," Geeko rallied everyone. "Joel and Naldo; you will stay with us in Coach's room, we will need you to help with the escape. Grace, Sam and Pixel; when you have all the Trackles, Pixel will fly back to the Enchanted Lodge and tell the Enchanted Alliance that the Trackles are safe and ask them to come to the Pearlball Pitch. Hopefully we should have the Weavers under control from then on."

"Just as a warning, Geeko. Pilates guy, Ferdinand, is a black belt in martial arts. Karate, Judo or Taekwondo. I can't remember which. Maybe all of them? He did this wooden plank breaking demonstration one afternoon on the ship. I was serving at the coffee bar at the time. It was quite a production with lots of noise, bravado and aggression. Apparently, he was banned from doing it again as it scared the old ladies. He was told to stick to Pilates." Naldo informed Geeko. "Ferdinand was quite put out. Rumor is he wore his martial arts uniform and black belt to the Pilates classes in protest. All the old ladies left scared and didn't come back. He was called into the Entertainment Director's office to explain himself. I think they threatened to kick him off the boat at the next port if he continued to scare passengers, so he stopped wearing martial arts clothing and went back to his usual tight leggings.

Anyway, just be careful everyone, he is a tough guy. Not the cleverest man on the planet, but he is strong."

The group looked around at each other. Admittedly, they were not the most intimidating group.

"Does anyone have any super powers?" Grace asked hopefully. "Magical talents? You are called magical folk after all?"

There was silence amongst the friends. Pixel was the first to answer.

"Hmm. I do wish that all those fairytale stories you humans read had been sent through the Enchanted Alliance first," said Pixel wistfully. "They are the cause of a lot of misunderstanding. Those Brother's Grimm were certainly 'grim' and sometimes downright wrong as to how they represented Magical folk. As for Walt Disney, what a great creative writer but that is what he was a creative writer; he was rather clueless in the lives of real Magical folk."

Stryker nodded in agreement, "We all have our talents and some of the talents can definitely be called magical. But carrying wands, casting spells and mixing potions in cauldrons are just not true."

"Yeah that would be weird." Pixel agreed. "Fairy Godmother's turning mice into horses. Pumpkins into carriages. Unrealistic and just plain weird."

"Let me try to explain," said Geeko patiently. "We have special talents depending on which type of Magical Folk you are born into. Gnomes are very intelligent. That is why they have larger heads than the other Folk and you rarely see them without a hat. Our heads are oddly shaped to house our bigger brains. They are very good at gadgets, coding, tech, planning strategies and inventing solutions out of the resources around them."

"Fairies, pixies and elves can fly, so that is magical and they each have special jobs. They inherit the special jobs and corresponding talents from their parents just like you do. Pixel, for example, inherited the talents needed for a tooth fairy from her parents. She can move very quietly which keeps her from waking the kids. Stryker can change her skin for Concealment tasks. Concealment is not only used to play Pearlball, it is used to hide them in times of danger. Other fairies like the flower fairies have skills to protect plants. Others protect animals. They are a complex type of folk, compassionate and helpful."

"Is Pixel compassionate and helpful ?" joked Joel. "I don't think so !!"

Pixel made a low growling noise. Then smiled back at Joel. "I don't have the talent to be kind and compassionate to humans. That would be a silly talent. Most humans don't deserve compassion at all."

Joel stuck out his tongue in reply. He knew she was talking about him.

Geeko continued, "Trolls who have a really bad rap in the human stories where they are portrayed as ugly and unfriendly, think Gringotts and the troll under the bridge. But truthfully, trolls are not mean like the humans portray them to be. They have a strong sense of loyalty and humor which makes them great guards and enforcers. Just because they are not the most attractive to look at, humans regard them as mean. Humans can be very shallow."

"Elves are the caregivers of the fairy world; they are the teachers, the doctors, nurses and the veterinarians. Their power is the ability to heal and nurture," Geeko continued. "Pixies are strong, quick and agile. They can fly for the longest time and can dodge through the sky like hummingbirds. I could go on but time is getting short. Basically, we all have magical powers but they are not as wishy-washy as shown in the books you read as kids. Life skills, helpful skills not outrageous made up skills. "

"So," summarized Sam, "Pixel can fly quietly, Stryker can hide and you Geeko can make cool tech things. Us humans are pretty useless, we can't help. What is the extent of our powers? I know we cannot help against a Blackbelt. Grace and I do Taekwondo at home, but we are only orange belts, blackbelt people are like the superheroes of martial arts. Or the bad guys with super powers in this case."

Grace agreed, "Are you sure we shouldn't just send Pixel back and wait for the Enchanted Alliance to come?"

"We can't wait," said Stryker sadly "The Weavers were talking about moving to another secret location. We can't risk losing the team."

"Also the longer the Magical world is without the Trackles. The more Magical Folk will remain in danger," Geeko added.

It was clear and everyone agreed; they had to act now.

"And don't forget." Geeko continued. "We have the combined talents of the Pearlball team too. Let me recap. Stryker tells me if I have got this right. Coach, the pixie, is strong, determined and agile. As far as I remember she is a unicorn pixie so she will also be able to summon Unicorns ... that could be very useful. Chuckle the gnome is the best goal scorer therefore very accurate and also strong. Becca the fairy, is the fastest on the team. Camio, the elf, is also gifted with the power of concealment. Greg and George, the troll brothers, are both strong and loyal. We have some good skills to work with."

"Hopefully Naldo won't have to use his Martial Arts on them." Joel added with his usual humor, breaking up the tension. "He is a blackbelt in origami. Maybe his paper napkin flowers can pass as nunchucks and we could throw them at the Weavers?"

Joel zoomed around the friends making whooshing air sounds pretending to make and throw origami nunchucks.

"Very funny," replied Naldo sarcastically. "Maybe your muscles formed by towel folding and pillow fluffing could be used to fluff the Weavers into submission?"

"Touche," agreed Joel, laughing. "Fair point."

He changed his air swooshing nunchuck actions into feeble punches making everyone laugh.

The group of friends refocused and listened. Grace and Sam felt a sense of belonging and purpose, which they had never felt so intensely before. They listened intently, as Geeko explained the rest of the plan. Stryker then added in some more details about the team and the building. It was a good plan. Maybe not completely without weakness or danger but Grace and Sam felt a little more optimistic by the end of the talk.

Time to put the plan into action.

Chapter 23

The Action

They moved towards the door. Grace felt nervous in the pit of her stomach and a little queasy. She was glad that she and Sam were staying outside and did not have to go inside.

Stryker directed them around the building to the coach's office window. Sam handed over the Magigad 3000 to Geeko, as he would need it to check where everyone was. They had a quick look at the screen together, everyone in the clubhouse was still in the commentary room. Two Weavers, Ferdinand and the Chef, were sitting on the white sofas. The team and Ms. Jessica were sitting on the floor in front of the commentators box while the third Weaver, Madame Cleaver, was wandering around amongst the team.

Pixel, Geeko, Stryker, Joel and Naldo made their way as planned to the door and using Coach's key, it opened easily. Grace and Sam watched as the group checked the Magigad once again to confirm that no one was close by the doorway and then entered. Before disappearing into the clubhouse, Geeko gave a nervous smile and a thumbs up to Grace and Sam, as the group disappeared into the building.

Sam felt strange without his Magigad. The Magigad had made him feel braver; he wished he still had it, but knew that Geeko would need it for his plan. Grace was also feeling weird as she realized this was the first time they had been alone on this adventure, just the two of them. She missed the others.

It felt like a long time, but really it was probably less than a minute before Geeko opened the window. Pixel popped up her head too, smiled and then presumably disappeared to find the Trackles. It was not long before she appeared back with a backpack presumably belonging to the coach.

"We can carry the Trackles in this," she whispered, passing it over "Plus it is super cool. Look, it is the original Pearlball merchandise," she pointed at a logo.

"We will have to make sure Coach gets it back," noted Stryker dutifully in the background.

"Shhh," hissed Naldo at the girls. "Geeko is turning on the stereo. Wish us luck. Everyone in their places."

Grace and Sam waited quietly in the grass. It was only a few minutes later that Pixel returned to the window. She had managed to locate the Trackles and she passed them through the window. Sam and Grace dutifully packed them into the backpack. Sam resisted the urge to examine them in detail, even though he was dying to see the Trackles close up. They turned towards the bleachers. But, that was when it all started to go wrong.

It was unclear to Grace and Sam what exactly had happened but they heard a loud buzzing sound from the coach's office then after a few seconds a frightened screech. It was unclear whose cry it was (maybe Stryker or Pixel).

Almost immediately Geeko's shadow came to the still open window, his white frightened face made a fleeting glance out. He had something in his hand, which he dropped down as carefully as he could into the long grass. Maybe another Trackle. He quickly closed the window shut and turned away.

Grace and Sam froze. This was not the plan. In the plan, Pixel would have flown out of the window and followed them to the Bleachers ready to take the Trackles to the Enchanted Alliance. The children were unclear what they should do. But someone had to do something.

"Make your way to the Bleachers, hide the bag and stay hidden," said Sam determinedly. "I'm going to get the other Trackle, which Geeko just dropped. Then I will follow you."

"Be careful," stammered Grace. She didn't really want to be separated from him, but had remembered that Geeko had emphasized how important it was to have all the Trackles. They didn't want any Trackles left behind. That was why Geeko had dropped it.

Grace turned in the other direction, carrying the heavy duffle bag. She slunk along, remaining hidden in the long grass, until she reached the assigned bleacher meeting place.

Sam took a deep breath and made his way quietly back to the window. He could hear voices above. He dropped down on his belly.

"No, we are alone," Geeko stuttered. Sam could tell by his voice he was scared but even so, he was thinking quickly. "We are the press. We came early for the game. Wwwe always check in with the coach before we go up to the commentary room and check the stereo. Whaat is going on? I don't understand ... Where is the coach?"

There were some bangs in the cupboards, then a rough voice responded, "You all come with me. Move it ... come on ..."

There were a lot of shuffling noises and a couple of protests followed by a slammed door.

Sam wriggled closer till he found the indented grass where the Trackle that Geeko had dropped had landed. Sam picked it up.

It was not another Trackle as Sam had thought, it was his Magigad, Sam was so relieved. He was not sure why but the Magigad made him feel safer and he was sure it would be useful. Plus, he was convinced that it would have been confiscated by the Weavers, therefore rendering it useless to them. Geeko had been smart and fast thinking to get it to him. Gnomes are obviously good at planning on the go.

Sam turned and with his Magigad safely stowed in his pocket, he ran towards Grace and the bleacher. He slowed as he got closer. He could hear voices from behind the seating. His heart dropped. Was Grace okay? Had someone got to the bleacher first and was waiting for them? He began to panic. As he took deep breaths and stopped to listen into the conversation. The voices were too calm to be Weavers and as he got closer he realized now one of the voices was Grace and the other was also familiar. It was Stryker.

Sam hurried to join them. Grace gave Sam a relieved hug. Both Grace and Stryker were happy to see him and were excited to see that Geeko had found a way to give them the Magigad back.

Stryker explained that she had escaped again by using concealment. She had been in Coach's room as the Weaver, Chef Claus, came down the stairs. "We were all with Geeko. Geeko was working on Coach's stereo so he could talk to the other team members through their ear phones. Pixel was about to leave to meet you. The stereo had been turned off so Pixel plugged it in and we were all waiting for it to power up. It turned on but reset to stereo mode, before Geeko could switch the plugs to earphone mode, the stereo had made this loud buzzy siren sound. Like an out of tune radio on full volume. Geeko had turned it off immediately and switched it to the earphone mode. But the noise had been more than loud enough to notify the Weavers that someone was in the building."

"Pixel screamed as she saw Chef Claus come down the stairs. Admittedly, he was an intimidating man, a large guy with a big black beard, black eyebrows which met in the middle and narrow squinty eyes. But Stryker added that she thought Pixel was merely warning them all with her scream that danger was approaching."

The warning had given Geeko enough time to drop the Magigad within reach of Sam and close the window. It had also given Stryker enough time to use concealment to hide against the wall.

Stryker watched as Chef Claus came in, made a quick sweep of the room and briskly hustled the others up the stairs. He had even looked right at Stryker but had not seen her. Chef Claus was more worried about the imposters which he had already found, so Stryker was left undiscovered. She waited a minute, then let herself out of the door and concealed herself across to the bleachers. The more direct route and being able to fly made her arrival at the bleachers well ahead of Sam and his more laborious route around the pitch in the long grass.

"We have to rescue them," Stryker begged, "This is all my fault. I talked them into helping rescue the team and now they are all prisoners, plus I just know that the Weavers are going to try to use them as hostages to get the tooth fairy powder. Or even worse. Oh, we have to try," Stryker was beside herself.

"Calm down," said Grace. She knew someone had to take control. But what were they to do?

"We have to get the word to the Enchanted Alliance that the Weavers are here and also return the Trackles as planned so that the Magical world can return to safety and normality as soon as possible. They will send help. That was Geeko's plan and we should stick to it," she concluded.

Sam agreed, "Stryker, you are the only one who can fly, so you have to go with the Trackles to the nearest safe zone and tell them to send some help."

"What about the others? We have to rescue them. They are bound to move everyone soon," argued Stryker.

"We will watch them on the Magigad Spy App. I know you will be fast and the more help we have, the better. In the meantime we will track that they do not leave and monitor that nothing bad happens"

"Okay, if you are sure," mumbled Stryker resignedly. "I will go as quickly as I can." She took the Trackles in the backpack and flew up through the grass away from the Pearlball pitch.

Grace and Sam looked at each other silently; it felt very lonely to be in this strange Magical world without any of their Magical friends.

Finally, Sam switched on the Magigad and turned it to solar power mode. Then they settled in a sunny spot, to see what was happening back in the clubhouse.

Chapter 24

Change of Plan

As Grace and Sam watched, there was a fair amount of movement in the club house. The hostages had been moved away from the front press room and back into an area. Luckily, Sam had made Stryker label the rooms; this room was labeled as the lunch room. It was upstairs at the far back of the clubhouse. Grace and Sam could see on the Magigad that in the room there were a few tables and chairs and some vending machines.

Ferdinand had moved off the plush white sofa in the press room and was now in the cafeteria too, standing at a vending machine and banging on the door, obviously trying to get something out.

Madame Cleaver and Chef Claus were also with him, walking around. Everyone else was sitting at a table. Sam quickly labeled Geeko, Pixel, Joel and Naldo so that they could be identified. Joel and Naldo were roughly the same height, so it was hard to know which was which but he guessed anyway. Everyone seemed to be looking at Madame Cleaver as though she was talking to them while she walked around. Except for Pixel who was staring out of the window.

"I wish we could hear what they are saying," Grace mused.

"We could try to get closer." Sam said hesitantly. He wasn't sure if he wanted to go closer but knew the Magigad's Electrophon would easily pick up the conversation if they did. "If we got right under the window, the Super Ear on the Spy App will pick up the conversation."

Grace was feeling brave in the knowledge that Stryker and the Enchanted Alliance would soon arrive and encouraged Sam to go closer.

"Let's go." she decided and started towards the clubhouse before she changed her mind.

The lunch room window was slightly ajar and though they could hear vague voices through the gap, it was only with the Super Ear App that they could actually hear what was being said. Sam fiddled with the volume and soon they could hear Madame Cleaver's New Jersey not French accent, through the headphones. Sam shared his EarPods with Grace and even though they only had one earpiece each, they could hear clearly.

"So, I repeat," she hissed. "We will be leaving in ten minutes. That pesky elf escaped somehow and is probably obtaining help. We are no longer safe here and we have found a new location where we can keep you. But we have a problem. We will be outside and some of you Magical People can fly or do other things which may jeopardize our mission. But those of you are the ones we need as hostages only through you will we be able to get to that magic powder. Therefore those of you who have wings, they will have to be clipped or cut off to stop you flying"

There was a frightened gasp from the group.

Ferdinand interrupted, "You are telling them too much," he snapped grumpily, taking over the conversation. "Claus, we need a vehicle. They won't be able to fly and we can't. Go look in the janitor's hut, there must be a lawnmower or something there - that pitch doesn't get cut on its own. We will cover ground faster if we ride on that. Madame, grab the Trackles and find something to tie these pests up with."

Ferdinand was obviously having some trouble with the vending machines as he shouted after her, "And find me some food."

The Weavers obviously did not know that the trackles were safely in the backpack on their way to the Enchanted Lodge with Stryker, Grace thought that was a good thing. But soon it would be revealed that the Trackles were gone. That was a bad thing.

Madame Cleaver and Chef Claus left.

Ferdinand started to prowl around the room growling under his breath. He wasn't nice when he was happy, but he was scary when he was hungry.

"Now, which of you lucky pests get to come with us as our bartering tools? Hmmmm, you for sure." he muttered, stopping by Coach. "If I take the Coach of the most well known and loved Pearlball team in the world, it is bound to get attention." He moved on and stopped by Pixel. "I have no idea who you are ... "The

Magigad map showed him leaning in towards her. "... But I smell toothpowder. Maybe I just found our very own Tooth Fairy." He laughed with an evil laugh like you hear in the films, "We will have to clip those silky wings though. Can't have you flying off on us like that other brat. Such a shame they are so pretty."

Pixel squealed.

Sam and Grace realized they had to act fast. They could not let Ferdinand cut Pixel's wings or any of their wings and if the Weavers left with the Coach and Pixel, they may never find them again. The Enchanted Alliance would arrive and everyone would be gone.

"We have to act now," Grace whispered. She looked around in the sky still hopeful of a rescue team. The sky was silent. A door banged at the front of the clubhouse. Claus was leaving for the Janitor's hut. "You go after that dude," Grace continued. "Try to lock him in or stall the lawnmower or something. I will try and stop the French teacher."

As she said that, they heard Coach's office door open.

They hugged each other quickly. And after a brief hesitation, Sam rushed off around the back of the club house to a garage-like building to the right which he hoped was the Janitor's hut. If he rushed he could get there first, as anyone coming from the clubhouse had to go around the Visiting Team Bleachers.

He sprinted towards the shed.

Chapter 25

A Little Drama and a Lot of Luck

As Sam ran, he tried to formulate a plan in his head. He decided his best bet would be to sabotage the lawnmower, then try to keep Chef Claus from returning to his fellow Weavers.

Sabotaging the lawnmower had to be his first mission. At least that would slow down their exit if nothing else.

But how was he to sabotage a lawnmower? Ride-on lawnmowers need keys and gas right? He had to either find and remove the key and/or remove the gas. Removing gas would be messy and could be dangerous. Plus he had no idea if a ride on a lawnmower had a key or a button to turn it on. As he turned the last corner and saw the door to the hut, he had a genius idea.

There on the side of the hut near to the door was a garden hose attached to a tap. Sam remembered one of his Chemistry lessons: Gas did not mix with water. If he could fill the gas tank with water, it would flood the engine and the lawnmower would not go anywhere. He had to be fast though. He turned the hose on and sprinted through the garage door, which was thankfully open, dragging the hose behind him. He located the gas cap on the huge green lawnmower, immediately opened it and began squirting water into the tank. He stopped only when he heard the front garage door opening. He stopped squirting the hose, threw it on the floor and hid behind the tool shop at the back of the hut.

Chef Claus entered grumbling and imitating Ferdinand.

"Go get the lawnmower. Do this, do that. Oh and get me some food! I need to feed my huge fat nose!" Obviously Chef Claus was not too happy with Ferdinand. "Well muscle guy, you got us into this mess. It wasn't me who lost the fairy girl. That was on your watch," Chef Claus did not seem to be in a rush.

This gave Sam time to look around.

He was behind a tool shop with hammers, nails, drills and the usual tools. By the door where he had entered, there were garden tools like brooms and rakes hung up neatly in a row. By the front garage door where Claus had entered, there was a smaller leaf blower, weedwacker and smaller push mower.

Next to the ride-on lawnmower was a ride-on roller, probably to keep the pitch flat. Sam sighed. He hoped Claus would not try to start that up. He hoped Claus would think it was too slow and therefore unlikely to be a good getaway vehicle. At the far back were some lawnmower attachments that looked like a snow shovel and leaf collector attachment.

Behind the lawnmower and roller, there was a storage area and in front of Sam, he could see the door to the restroom. The door was open and he could see inside. He turned back to Claus, who was still moaning about Ferdinand.

He was comically pushing the smaller push mower. "I'll bring you a lawnmower, Dummkopf this one won't get you far. Brum Brmm," He laughed at his own joke and fake lawnmower noise. Smiling now, he moved over to the ride-on roller. He jumped on the seat.

"Oh no," thought Sam, "not the roller".

"Hey Ferdi! This machine has a roller the size of your nose. Hope you don't get a cold anytime soon or we will have to clear your conk out using the snow blower."

Claus was having too much fun with his pretend conversation.

Sam was glad as it gave him time to think. He was doubly glad when Chef Claus moved off the roller and onto the lawnmower. Sam had a plan. He took his opportunity and snook out carefully from behind the tool shop and pulled the key from the inside of the restroom door.

"Puddles," muttered Chef Claus, accidentally stepping in the water by the gas tank and shaking his foot. He looked up, "This place must have a leaky roof."

Sam used Chef Claus's distraction as his opportunity; he grabbed the hose and maneuvered to the front by the garage door. He flicked the hose to jet spray and began to shoot Chef Claus with it, being careful to hold the jet spray at such an angle that Chef Claus could not see him, this meant basically spraying him in the face.

"Plegh, plugh, flarr," Chef Claus made some loud exclamations as the water pelted him in the face. Sam's plan was working, Claus was backing up towards the restroom.

It reminded Sam of a fairground game he and Grace had played last spring. You held a water jet and had to spray a ball up a wall, through a maze and finally into a hole at the top. Sam angled the jet spray to the right and left until Claus was right outside the restroom. Claus did exactly what Sam had hoped he looked for, Claus saw the safety of the restroom. He jumped in and slammed the door shut behind him, stopping the barrage of water. Sam did not hesitate. He dropped the hose and locked the door with the key he had retrieved earlier and added a broom wedged in the door handle for extra measure.

Success. But Sam did not have time to gloat; he had to get back to help Grace. On his way back, he thankfully noted that the outside window to the restroom was tiny. No way plump Chef Claus was getting out that way.

Chapter 26

Galant Grace

Meanwhile, Grace had been assessing the situation from the window outside the coach's office. Madame Cleaver was already inside and looking around frantically.

"Where are those Trackles?" Madame Cleaver muttered. "I'm sure we left them in the drawer. Maybe Ferdie moved them when he came down with the fairy. He could have told me," she complained.

She threw everything out of the drawer and onto the floor. "Well they are not there." She turned her attention to the locker on the right, where Stryker had hidden earlier. It was a large locker full of coats and odd gym equipment. It would take Madame Cleaver a while to search as it was dark and she did not have a light.

Grace had to get in the room. She could see that the keys to the office were outside the door on the floor. She crossed her fingers that the front door to the clubhouse was still open.

As fast, yet as quietly as she could, she turned the corner to the front door, ducking to avoid being seen through the other window.

A strike of luck: the door was open. She took a deep breath and entered the clubhouse lobby looking around, trying to remember the layout of the clubhouse from the Magigad map which Stryker had labeled. The door to Coach's office was on the left, restrooms were on the right, then there was a small corridor to the stairs and the elevator. To the left of the elevator was the cleaning trolley. Stryker had pointed that out when she recognized Ms Jessica, the cleaning lady. The cart was filled with her cleaning supplies. Grace had to think fast.

She grabbed the cart and wheeled it in front of her, pulling some dusters and a tin of carpet deodorizer off the front compartment as she did. Feeling partly protected behind the cleaning supply cart, she bravely pushed the door to Coach's office open.

Madame Cleaver heard her enter. She backed out of the locker and turned looking confused. She was immediately showered by a cloud of carpet deodorizing powder, which Grace had dusted into the air. Coughing as the highly perfumed cloud fell onto her from above, Madame Cleaver did the only thing she could, she returned into the locker for fresher air. Grace, who had tied a duster over her nose and head so she would not be affected by the powder, hurriedly closed the door on her and wedged a mop in it, keeping it firmly closed. "My hair, my hair, it will ruin my hair." Grace could hear her shouting in her thick New Jersey accent, along with some banging between the hangers. Grace did not wait any longer; she was not sure how long the wedged mop would last. She unwrapped the dusters from her head and nose and wondered what she should do next. Should she find Sam? Should she head outside?

Then, she heard noise upstairs.

"What is going on?" demanded Ferdinand from the room above. "Get up here Cleaver. Bring some scissors or a knife so I can slit open the fairy's wings"

"*Time to get the cleaning supply cart back,*" Grace thought. "*It had proven useful before and it was somehow comforting to have it in front of her.*" She ran back into the office. Madame Cleaver was banging on the door of the locker now and sneezing occasionally. "Is someone there?" she pleaded. "Let me out. Aaaaachoo. My hair is covered in this stuff..."

Grace grabbed the cart and ran back out. It took a little longer this time to lock the door as her hands trembled in excitement. She turned and looked at what was left on the cart.

Furniture polish, floor wax, a mop, broom, bucket, more dusters, cleaning solution, a tin of metal polish, rubber gloves, dustpan and brush and some sponges.

She figured Ferdinand would be reluctant to leave the group and come to see what the noise was about, as he was all alone upstairs guarding the others. But at some point he might. For now, she had to keep him upstairs.

Grace jumped as the door behind her, which led onto the pearlball pitch opened. For a split second as the light shone in, she froze thinking it was Chef Claus but as the figure moved closer, she saw Sam rather wet but smiling. She had never been happier to see her brother. She flung her arms around him and hastily issued instructions.

Chapter 27

Shiny ending?

"Floor wax," stated Grace simply.

"Excuse me," answered Sam "Four whacks? What or who are we whacking?"

"No Sam. We are not hitting anything. I said 'Floor wax' not 'Four whacks'. We have to wax the stairs," continued Grace hastily.

Sam was still confused, on the scale of tidiness Grace was certainly ranging on the tidy side but cleaning was not really her thing. Why would she think of that now?

"Floor wax. It will make the stairs slippy," Grace explained, feeling a little frustrated at Sam's blank expression. "It will stop that Ferdie Guy from getting down the stairs. May even make him fall so we can push him into the team restroom and lock the door?"

"What about the elevator? He could come down that way?" questioned Sam. Grace hesitated clearly thinking this through. "He does seem a little lazy for a gym instructor."

"Hmmm. Watch this," exclaimed Grace, pressing the button to summon the elevator. She crossed her fingers that the noise of the elevator would not be heard by Ferdinand. When the elevator arrived Grace hopped in, pressed the button to go up to the next floor, quickly hopped out and wedged a bucket in-between the doors so it couldn't close.

"That elevator is not going anywhere if it cannot not close the door," Grace said proudly. "Safety feature ... to stop people getting crushed."

It started beeping dramatically and the doors kept closing and opening again as they got close to the bucket.

"Genius," commented Sam adding another bucket and sponges to ensure there was no way the elevator doors could ever close.

"Let's polish," said Grace, handing Sam a duster covered in the wax. They rushed around the corner to the stairs. There was certainly some commotion going on upstairs, but no one was in the hallway.

"Let's wax from the eighth step downwards so we don't slip," noted Sam wisely. They went halfway up and frantically started dusting the wax onto the wooden stairs and reversing down each step.

"How do we get him down?" asked Sam frantically polishing stair number three.

"We will have to use ourselves as bait. Quick hide. I hear someone coming," replied Grace in a hushed whisper.

They grabbed the cleaning supplies, pushed the cleaning supply cart to the bottom of the stairs and hid behind the banister. They could hear Ferdinand upstairs; he seemed to be getting more and more enraged.

He opened the door, stuck his head out of the cafeteria and looked down the stairs. He shouted frustratedly, "Where are you Cleaver? You are taking way too long. Hurry up! Claus, Cleaver ..." He was getting more desperate as time passed and now the door was open he could probably hear the elevator beeping.

As Ferdinand became distracted, upstairs went crazy. Geeko, Pixel, Naldo and Joel had indicated to the others to move. Geeko had issued instructions to the team fast. Somehow, he had recalled all of their attributes.

"Chuckle, you are the team's best goal scorer, run around to the gym and grab the exercise balls. Camio, conceal yourself and stand behind Ferdinand. Chuckle, throw the balls to Camio, Camio will throw them at Ferdinand. Let's try to keep Ferdinand out of the room while I open the window. Coach, you are strong; help me and Naldo push the vending machine across the door just in case Ferdinand heads back here. Joel, open the window as wide as you can. Fairy folk must escape first through the window before Ferdinand comes back and potentially slits your wings. Protect your Chitin. Becca, you are the fastest to go and get help. George and Greg, follow Chuckle and grab anything you can, to throw at Ferdinand."

The brothers followed Chuckle through the computer room and grabbed the seat cushions from the sofas and started throwing them at Ferdinand, who had now made his way closer to the stairs. They looked around for heavier items.

Meanwhile, Chuckle had found the largest exercise ball from the gym and threw it accurately to Camio, who had flown above Ferdinand. She had concealed to the exact color of the ceiling. She caught the ball effortlessly and aimed it hard onto Ferdinand's huge nose. The momentum and weight of the ball and his nose were enough to make him swivel, trip and fall down the stairs. Halfway down, he grabbed the banister to steady himself, but slipped on the perfectly polished, slick stairs. He crashed to the bottom, landing nose first on top of the cleaning supply cart which Grace and Sam had strategically left there.

Sam and Grace, spotting their opportunity, rushed out from their hiding spot and pushed the cart into the restroom with Ferdinand laying stunned on top. It took both of them to push him. They left him there, still wedged in the cart between the toilet bowl and sink. They locked the door securely behind them.

They were so fast that Ferdinand had not realized what had happened. Sam was sure Ferdinand must have been still seeing stars from his fall and he would certainly have a fair few bruises and a very sore nose.

They returned to the stairs to greet the team members and warned them to be careful on the polished stairs.

"I have never seen them so shiny." complimented Ms Jessica the Cleaner. As she, like the others, held the rail on the way down, those with wings opened the window and left from there as planned.

"Dangerously clean," joked Joel. "Excellent," he dramatically slid down the banister to hug the kids.

Geeko was a little more conservative when he got down the stairs. "Where are the Weavers?" he asked, looking around nervously.

Naldo followed Joel's example and slid down the rails and high-fived the kids.

Sam reassured Geeko about the location of the Weavers. "Two in the restroom and one hanging around with the hangers in the Coach's locker," he revealed proudly.

"Ferdinand is in the restroom," Grace confirmed. "Powdering his nose," she joked.

"The Chef is toweling himself off in the Janitor's hut restroom," Sam added. "He got a little wet and I had to wash off his bad attitude."

"And Madame Cleaver is hidden in the closet worrying about the fragrance of her hair," laughed Grace mimicking a French accent for 'fragrance of her hair.'

Chapter 28

Praise indeed

They were laughing in the lobby, while Chuckle and the brothers made sure there was no way Madame Cleaver or Ferdinand could escape, when they heard a noise outside.

Grace peered nervously out of the window. It was not that she didn't trust her brother, but for some reason, she thought Chef Claus still may be making a reentrance. Bad attitude and all.

She was wrong. It was a happy sight to see. She called the others over.

Pixel was reunited with Stryker and they were flying around the pitch swooping and diving together like beautiful tropical birds. They stopped their flight suddenly as they noticed a beautiful deer at the far end of the pitch. The majestic animal towered over the Oyster Shell Goals; it bent one of its knees to the ground and laid its head on the perfectly mown pitch in front of it. A group of about ten trolls, wearing the same Enchanted Alliance uniforms, which Grace and Sam had seen back at the Enchanted lodge, efficiently slid down the deer's neck and landed on the pitch looking around them. They were holding thick sticks and each had a square electronic device hung around their neck. They looked quite intimidating.

They motioned behind them and other Magical Folk, who also descended from the patiently kneeling deer.

The last one to descend was much smaller in height, but looked much more official. He was a gnome with a super long beard, which made him look like a miniature wizard, like Dumbledore, this was emphasized by the fact that he wore a long black cape and hat with a gold trim which shone in the sunlight. The Trolls formed a circle around the gnome, who turned to the deer and stroked her nose. The deer then slowly raised her head and lopped off majestically back through the grass.

The group looked tense as they moved hesitantly across the pitch; the trolls encircling the gnome and looking around them in all directions.

"That's Professor Elk, the most important member of the Enchanted Alliance. I think they think the Weavers are still in control judging by their serious faces," whispered Geeko in awe.

As they watched, Pixel and Stryker swooped down to greet the Enchanted Alliance members. The trolls at first startled and formed a tighter ring around Professor Elk. They spoke to Stryker and Pixel, then encircled them too. They headed cautiously towards the clubhouse door.

"Come on," said Geeko with the excited voice of a child who was about to meet his pop star idol. "We have to tell them it's okay," he rushed down the stairs to open the doors. The sound of

Madame Cleaver banging still coming from the office. "My hair, my hair, my beautiful hair," she wept.

Geeko, Grace, Sam, Naldo and Joel bounded out of the door and towards the circle of trolls. Geeko led the way, smiling from ear to ear, starstruck at the thought of meeting his hero, Professor Elk.

The trolls, not knowing Geeko and seeing a group of mini humans (Grace, Sam, Naldo and Joel) advancing towards them at a pace, became alarmed; they made the circle tighter around the Professor, Pixel and Stryker. The electronic device around their neck lit up and flashed. In sequence, they pointed their sticks up in the air and then directly towards the approaching group.

Geeko screeched to a halt seeing the aggressive stance of the trolls.

"Woah," he shouted "No, we are friendly," he cautioned, motioning for the others to stay back. Trolls could be extremely aggressive, especially when they felt they or their friends could be threatened. That was what made them extremely good bodyguards. They were not to be messed with.

Pixel suddenly popped up from behind the wall of trolls.

"Wait," she called the trolls. "They are with us. They are not the Weavers. They are the ones who found the Trackles and sent Stryker to you," Pixel escaped the troll circle and flew out to greet her friends.

"Where are the Weavers? Did we rescue everyone?" asked Pixel, who was unaware of what had happened in her absence.

"Everything's fine, " Geeko filled her in, a little embarrassed about the misunderstanding. He had been too starstruck to realize that he had put them all in danger. It must have seemed as though the Weavers were coming, especially as he was sure the Enchanted Alliance knew the Weavers were human, not magical folk and Grace, Sam, Joel and Naldo were obviously human.

"The Weavers are all secure," Geeko continued. "The team is safe."

Right on cue, almost as though they could hear him, the entire Pearlball team came out of the clubhouse across the pitch to meet them. They were led by coach who had summoned everyone back using the stereo and ear pieces.

The trolls, seeing the Pearlball team approaching, smiling from ear to ear, relaxed. They waited until they had Professor Elk and coach's confirmation that all was indeed well, allowed Professor Elk to walk through their protective circle, towards the friends and team. Stryker followed behind squeezing through the gap left by the trolls. Finally, Geeko got to meet the Professor and he looked very happy indeed.

Professor Elk shook everyone's hand and thanked them for all their efforts. He listened as Geeko described what had happened; Joel and Naldo described who the Weavers were and Grace and Sam filled him in on where they were currently located.

"It seems you have done superb work my friends," Professor Elk observed, after listening carefully to all the events. "The magical world is indebted to you. Thank you. You are indeed brave, honest citizens and friends of our world. The Trackles are in safe hands and are all being reprogrammed by our tech team. We can reopen the safe zones and the Magical Folk can go on with life as usual. The Pearlball team are not only a group of wonderful people, but their sport represents a mix of all magical folk working in unity. It is a symbol of our entire magical world working together as one. You have made our world safe and reunited us as one. You are heroes indeed."

When he mentioned the word 'heroes'; one of the Trolls stepped forward and took out what seemed to be a camera.

"Picture, Sir?" he asked respectfully.

"Certainly Herold. Good idea," answered Professor Elk. He leaned forward and posed with the group. Everyone smiled broadly. Herold earnestly took the photo with a bright flash.

Professor Elk returned to his usual more serious pose, "Now we must clear up the mess that these meddling Weavers have caused and return the Magical World to normal business. We have been disrupted long enough. Thank you again friends."

He turned to the group.

"Chuckle, please take the trolls to the locations of the Weavers. They will secure them and bring them to me."

Led by a beaming Chuckle, the trolls walked towards the club house and then towards the janitor's shed.

Chapter 29

Time Crunch

Professor Elk left with the last couple of trolls towards the clubhouse. The group of friends were soon joined by the Pearlball team and Ms. Jessica, the cleaner. Everyone was very thankful that the rescue had been made and Ms. Jessica really enjoyed hearing about how important her cleaning cart had been.

"That is a story I will be talking about for many years. I always knew my work was important," she laughed.

They all agreed, but were interrupted by a loud buzzing sound.

The sound seemed to be coming from Naldo. Pixel jumped and made a squeak, "What is that noise for? " she frowned at Naldo as though he had made the noise just to frighten her, "I have heard enough loud noises today, Naldo ..."

Grace and Sam had jumped too, but they both remembered what was happening. Naldo's watch alarm was going off.

"We only have a half hour to get back," answered Grace, nervously. "Naldo set the alarm so we would know when we had to head back to the Brilldom."

"Right." confirmed Naldo "We had better be in our way. Geeko do you see any seeds to surf on?

Geeko did not even look around.

"Well even if I did," he noted, raising his finger in the air, "It would not get us back to the ship. The wind is blowing the wrong way and we would end up inland not towards the sea. We will have to go by foot. Even the best seed surfer cannot guide their pod opposite the direction of the wind."

Grace started to panic. They had surfed on the pods a long way here; it would take them much longer to walk all that way even if they went really fast. At their present height, they couldn't cover any ground fast.

"Does anyone have a Trackle?" asked Joel. "Maybe we could summon a friendly animal to run us to the port."

"All the Trackles are being reprogrammed back at the Enchanted Lodge," Stryker told them. "They said it would take a few hours to re-sync them so I left them all there."

Sam and Grace looked at each other. Things were not looking good for catching the cruise ship before it left the port. They knew the ship did not wait for passengers or crew.

A quiet but assured voice answered.

"I can help," It was Coach. " I am a Unicorn Elf. I can summon a unicorn. They can at least take you to the Enchanted Lodge. It's the least I can do to thank you."

Unicorns!! Grace had become accustomed to magical folk but not unicorns? Unicorns didn't really exist right? How come humans had never seen them? Imagine horses running all over with a horn in the middle of their heads, there was never a chance that they would not be spotted.

Grace's questions and disbelief were soon challenged. Coach made a motion with her fingers in her mouth, as though she was about to whistle. She seemed to whistle loudly but not a sound came from her mouth, or at least not one Grace or Sam could hear.

Seconds later, Grace was startled again, this time by the fact that the advancing unicorns made no noise. They were as radiant and beautiful as she imagined as a child, but much smaller. In fact, at Grace and Sam's current height, the unicorns looked horse size. But they were their current size, therefore no way they could be seen by humans. Their ears did not reach above the grass. They galloped effortlessly and silently across the Pearlball pitch towards them, stopping abruptly in front of the group, air steaming from their noses, their coats like glittery suede and their distinctive horns protruding out from between their ears a most impressive sight indeed.

Grace had thought the oyster Pearlball goals were an amazing color and texture, but they were nothing in comparison to the unicorn's horns. Their horns were a rainbow of colors, different at every angle, twisted in shape like the auger seashells Sam and Grace had collected last year at the beach.

The spiral shape made a kaleidoscope of colors out of the reflections of light around them. The hair from their splendid forelocks and manes, washed over the colors like the tide from a gentle sea, ebbing and flowing in unison with the unicorns movement.

Just like horses, the unicorns were all unique in size, height and color combinations. They looked splendid. Joel and Naldo had obviously never seen a unicorn before either, as they also gasped in amazement.

"Wow. They are splendidly, excellent," stuttered Joel in amazement.

Coach walked forward and stroked the beautiful creatures, who nudged her gently with their muzzles all patiently waiting for her touch. She gently stroked them and explained to the group that she was a coach in her spare time, but in her real capacity, she was a unicorn elf, elves are the carers of the Magical world, the teachers, the nurses, the vets. Coach must be the guardian and caregiver for unicorns. Judging by their gentle loving demeanor towards her, the unicorns obviously loved Coach. Her touch and voice calmed them. As she stroked them, she whispered in a strange language to them.

"They will take you to the port," smiled Coach. "They move as a herd so there are more than plenty for you to ride. Take your pick."

Joel, Naldo, Sam, Geeko and Pixel chose their unicorn carefully. The process reminded Sam of choosing a spot on a carousel ride. He looked around and chose a tall, handsome looking one with kind eyes. As Sam walked over to stroke him, the unicorn knelt down like a camel, letting Sam mount on top with ease. The unicorn waited patiently for him to get his seat, then rose gently from his knees, back to full height.

Pixel ran and gave Stryker a hug before she chose her unicorn. Whispering in her ear that when she came through the Enchanted lodge she needed to give her and the team's signature to a very friendly elf on the desk, just as they had promised.

"I know I can fly but I really want to ride a unicorn. Do you think they will still play the Pearlball match?" Pixel asked her friend.

"I think so," replied Stryker looking over at Coach.

"I am sure it will be delayed so the Weavers can be removed safely," Coach agreed. "After the Weavers have left, the game will no doubt be rescheduled. It is, after all, the biggest Pearlball tournament of the year. The other team and spectators will arrive, as soon as they are told they can leave the safe zones."

"What will happen to the Weavers?" asked Grace, looking back at the clubhouse where Ferdinand, Chef Claus and Madame Cleaver were being led out of the building by the trolls. Their hands were tied behind their backs and they looked miserable, Ferdinand was complaining loudly, trying to kick the troll who was leading him. The troll seemed completely unfazed and simply held his hand on Ferdinand's nose and walked ahead; Ferdinand's legs could not reach out far enough beyond his nose to do any kicking. It looked comical, Ferdinand's red nose still huge and red from his fall earlier. His useless karate kicks threw him slightly off balance each time.

"Oh, the Enchanted Alliance will take them and recharge their brain waves to forget the events and eventually return them to their normal size. But no chance they will make the cruise ship in time. They will lose their jobs for sure. Maybe they will even reset their brains to be nice in future." Geeko informed them.

"If they can find their brains," commented Joel cheekily, mounting on his chosen unicorn a smaller, sweet looking one with a bright pink mane "How do you know all this stuff Geeko?"

"Well," exclaimed Geeko, noting that the others were looking at him like he was crazy that he should know all this. "It was simply in the Geomechanical Magic Magazine about The Enchanted Alliance. January 17th, Article 7, Edition 12. It was an interesting discussion on the ethics of when the Enchanted Alliance were justified in using the very powers we are talking about. A decision was agreed upon unanimously, that means without a doubt, by all Enchanted Alliance Council members. I think there will be no disagreement in this case."

"Do you read that cover to cover every week?" asked Pixel.

"Yep," answered Geeko simply. "Twice."

They all turned to look. A dark shadow covered them for a second and there was a brief, but strong, gust of wind.

Whatever had arrived to take the Weavers was so fast. It looked like a blur as it landed next to the Magical Coalition Entourage.

"A Merlin," observed Stryker in awe. "It is related to the Peregrine Falcon and can fly as fast as 200 mph. Disputably the fastest bird on earth. Beautiful isn't it?"

Sam noted its beautiful markings and regal look. It was beautiful but had a slightly scary bird of prey look to it. He was glad he had a magical unicorn to get him home.

Geeko continued, "You are right Stryker. The Merlin can fly extremely fast and has been chosen as the guardian of the Enchanted Alliance; it can get them places fast and also naturally scares away swallows. You won't see a swallow within a 10 mile radius of a Merlin. If you did it would be a very unlucky swallow. It is the Merlin's favorite choice of food. The bird was named after Merlin, the famous wizard, who kept them as pets and gave them magical powers to help protect and assist Magical Folk. All the Merlins were probably busy with helping magical folks find safe zones when the coalition arrived. They were a natural choice as they are so fast. I would love to ride one."

As he spoke, the beautiful bird had loaded the group Weavers, Trolls and Professor Elk onto its broad back and rose gracefully into the sky.

As they watched it disappear. Geeko said "We had better be on our way too. Goodbye friends," he said to the Pearlball team. They hugged, expressed their thanks and waved goodbye.

Geeko had taken Coach's advice and chosen a majestic looking unicorn. Coach had whispered in his ear that he must be the leader of the herd. This was confirmed as when he turned and rose into the air first and the other unicorns followed.

"Bye," shouted Pixel waving at the team below who were all waving back. "Good luck in the match."

"Thank you," they shouted in reply.

Gradually, the Pearlball pitch faded out of view and soon the friends could see the ocean in the distance spread out like a tablecloth of blue in front of them.

Chapter 30

Forty-five Seconds of Fame

The unicorns were an experience which Grace and Sam would never forget. They were so graceful and smooth. Unlike a horse, they seemed to glide rather than gallop, their rhythmic swaying was actually more like a carousel ride than a horse ride. Even though the unicorn gait had seemed slow and smooth, they had covered the ground from the Pearlball pitch to the port incredibly fast. Much faster than by seedsurfing.

The ocean came closer and they could see The Brilldom in front of them, its wide decks came into focus and the children could see little figures moving around on the deck and pool area.

The unicorns landed as Coach had instructed, just short of the port gates in the long grass by the road to the port. The Unicorns politely knelt down so the friends could dismount, then as a herd, rose back up and returned back in the direction they had come from.

"That was fun," Grace noted, sighing.

"Radically, excellent," confirmed Joel.

The relaxed, magical feeling attained from flying the beautiful unicorns did not last long. There was a loud noise which grew super loud really fast. Geeko pushed them to move, as a huge black object passed them by. Grit was thrown from the road by the noisy machine. The grit flew through the air into the grass narrowly missing Naldo. The group startled and ran deeper into the grass. The grit was as big as rocks.

"This way," yelled Geeko over the noise. Sam had not heard and was running in the opposite direction. Pixel flew swiftly after him and tugged on his collar to redirect him.

In a matter of seconds, another huge black object rolled by sending more grit into the grass. The group of friends rolled behind a grassy mound and sat panting on the other side, covering their ears from the noise. There was a short break in action, but they could hear another machine approaching them.

"What are they?" shouted Grace.

"The grit is being thrown up from the cruise buses returning from the day trip," answered Geeko. "Your parents will be on one. Don't worry, it will take them a while to unload and get through security, but we will have to keep moving to get there first. Follow me."

He ran to a certain spot where he moved some moss and revealed a silver door. He entered a code and explained that they were back at the Enchanted lodge entrance; the door slid open. Two trolls were guarding the entrance from the inside. Geeko greeted the trolls and as directed put his hand onto a sensor, presumably so they could check his identity, but the trolls laughed.

"You guys rescued the Pearlball team right?" The first troll asked. "You managed to return the Trackles and capture the Weavers. You don't need to take the Identification test. Your pictures are all over the screens. You are heroes, dudes."

The other troll smiled and shook their hands, as he opened the last security door, which led into the Enchanted Lodge reception area. The familiar white desks, walls laden with huge nature photos and white sofas were just the same as when they had left. However, the Magical Folk were not running around scared. They sat chatting on the sofas or standing around talking, but the talking stopped as the group of friends entered. They stared at the incoming group. They obviously had seen their faces on the screens too. They started cheering, clapping and high-fiving the friends, making a gap for them, as they made their way through towards Aunt V.'s doorway.

They felt like movie stars arriving at a show. The admiring fans multiplied as the word spread of their entrance. Their way was lined by a crowd. They shook hands and worked their way smiling through the huge room. As they got to the door, they turned and waved and disappeared into the quiet of Aunt V's elevator.

"Well that was weird," observed Naldo, smiling as Geeko pressed the button to go down.

"That was excellent," said Joel, as he looked at his watch, "45 seconds of fame." He bowed theatrically, "I feel like a superstar."

Grace and Sam were grinning too.

"Would have been fun to stay longer," noted Sam "I have always wanted to give out autographs."

Pixel rummaged around in her backpack, found a piece of paper and passed it to Sam.

"Please sir? Can I have your autograph?" she joked.

The group were still laughing and pretending to take photos of each other when the elevator stopped and the door opened.

Aunt V. rushed forward to meet them.

"You are all such heroes." she gushed. "You have been all over the Geomechanical Magic website and on all the screens. I am so proud. Just think of my little Geeko and his friends, famous and celebrated by the Enchanted Alliance. It is so exciting. I have been knitting like crazy to celebrate."

She motioned to her desk. Above which was a colorful knitted banner saying, "WELCOME BACK HEROES." It really was quite impressive.

"And I made you some medals," she informed them, picking up a bunch of wool from her desk. They unwound into six intricately knitted medals made of gold wool and looped around with red ribbon. None of them had ever seen a knitted medal before, it was a rather strange concept but they were all far too polite to say anything but, "Thank you Aunt V." as she ceremoniously placed them around their necks.

Geeko hugged his Aunt. "Aunt V," he said "These are marvelous and I must say I am so excited to hear about being on the Geomechanical Magic Website, but we really have to rush to get everyone back on board before the Brilldom leaves."

"Oh, yes of course," agreed Aunt V. She hugged everyone then she tapped her knitting needle on her desk and it once again transformed into a wand which she waved at a door. The door opened and she motioned for them to enter, stating, "The Airflush chamber. The numbers have been reversed and you should all have an enjoyable trip back to your own size and back to the Brilldom. It has been a pleasure to meet you Grace and Sam. The entire Magical Kingdom and I personally are so glad you came. Thank you."

"Yes Aunt V.," agreed Geeko. "We really could not have done it without them. We will have to fill you in on all the details next time."

"Oh I am sure I will read all about it when the Geomechanical Magic Magazine interviews you. Oh, I can't wait till the next Mibbage meeting everyone is going to be asking me so many questions."

"Mibbage is like Cribbage but magical. Aunt V. and my Mom go every Tuesday evening with a bunch of their friends." Pixel filled them in.

Grace and Sam were not sure what cribbage or mibbage were, but nodded anyway.

"Pixel, make sure you take the leftist route. Otherwise you will end up human size," Mrs V warned as she hugged Pixel.

"Oh can I go human sized? Please Aunt V? Just once?" she begged.

Aunt V. laughed. "Always asking. Pixel, I don't think the passengers of the Brilldom would take well to a human sized fairy with wings. They would drop you off at the next zoo. Stick to the plan, love." She giggled.

With that she closed the door behind her and they got ready to leave the Port of Enchantment.

Chapter 31

Returning to Normal

Inside the room were two tubes. Geeko quickly explained to Grace and Sam what was going to happen, "These are the reverse portals. They are programmed to take you up to the air flush, which will make you back to your correct size. It will feel as though you are taking a very powerful shower, but it is actually a powerful air compression chamber combined with the anti-equation-uniform-berzoras, which combine to make the scantopia's react; therefore causing the body cells to grow. It does not hurt and you probably won't even notice you have grown until you are back at the Centrifugal Porthole."

"You lost me at 'anti-equation," admitted Joel. "But he's right, kids, it doesn't hurt at all. Watch out for the last spin as we hit the Centrifugal Porthole. It will throw us up into the laundry room, don't stick out your arms. Keep them into your body until you hit the floor. I smashed a watch once. Did not even notice until I was folding towels that evening."

"Lastly," concluded Geeko. "I really want to thank you again for all your help, for the rescue of the Pearlball team and also for rescuing us. We could not have done it without you. It has been a real pleasure."

He stuck out his arm to shake Grace and Sam's hands, then hugged them both.

"It has been such good fun," confirmed Pixel. "And I got to do my most spectacular rescues on you 'Sam the Swallow Scarer'. I think you may still have been floating along seed surfing had I not been there. I know the International Tooth Depot will want to thank you both too, for saving the Tooth Powder, that would have been tragic if the Weaver's had got hold of the powder. Oh, and I personally want to thank you for saving my wings. I was super scared that Ferdi guy was going to slit them. I am really going to miss you guys," she hugged them both, her eyes tearing up a little.

"We will see you again sometime right ?" Sam said quietly. He was not ready to say goodbye for good.

"Oh, don't worry." Joel said cheerfully. "We will find an excuse to bring you out on an adventure before the cruise is finished. Maybe even tomorrow. Pixel always cries when she says goodbye to us too."

"Do, so not," replied Pixel.

"Oh, that is not true Pixel," Geeko observed. "You wouldn't let Naldo and Joel go the first time they left. You made them promise they would come back the next day. Remember."

"Only because Naldo promised to bring me some breakfast waffles." Pixel said grinning.

"Waffles, bacon, muffins and eggs, actually," confirmed Naldo, "She found out I worked on the breakfast line."

He affectionately hugged her too.

"Get going," she said jokingly, hugging him back and smiling.

Time to go for real now. They stepped into the tubes. Geeko and Pixel in the one on the left and Joel, Naldo, Grace and Sam in the one on the right. A few seconds later and whoosh; Joel, Naldo, Grace and Sam, were back in the laundry room.

The way back was as much fun and as fast as the way down. Grace's hair was a little crazier than normal when she arrived in the laundry room. Geeko was right; it felt like they had been in a very powerful shower or maybe like the time they had been in the hurricane simulation at the science museum followed by a crazy tornado spin.

They had no idea how they had actually got back to the laundry room and Geeko was not there to explain. Sam thought to himself he would probably not be able to understand him, even if he did explain it. The washing machine door was open but no one had any recollection of coming through it. Strange. It must have been because they were dizzy from the spinning.

"Excellent. We made it back with just about the right amount of time. Maybe a few minutes early even," Joel looked at Naldo's watch.

"Grace and Sam climb on the washing machine. We will shove you back up through the trapdoor above back into the Fizzy and

Busy Club storeroom. If anyone sees you or asks, just say you fell asleep in there. No one will worry, people fall asleep in all kinds of places on the cruise ship. Especially the oldies. They found one in the larder just before breakfast. Scared the maid to bits when she went in to load her tray for breakfast orders. I am pretty sure the guy had become peckish in the night, found the food and had fallen asleep. Bet he won't do that again though, I am sure. The maid screaming for the cruise security, then being interrogated about how much had been eaten was not a wonderful way to wake up., Naldo explained.

"Hey Grace you look a little taller." said Joel observantly. "Look, you are a good two inches taller than Sam now.

Sam looked up at his sister smiling, "Must have been Aunt V."

Grace smiled.

Joel and Naldo hoisted Grace up onto the washing machine. She opened the trapdoor and scrambled back under the shelf. Sam followed.

"Bye," Joel called. "See you in the gangway."

"Bye," Naldo called. "See you at dinner."

Chapter 32

Reunited

Grace and Sam heard the slam of the laundry room door, as Naldo and Joel rushed back to the staff quarters and on to their tasks.

Grace and Sam were left coughing with dust in the dark. Sam fumbled in his pocket for the Magigad and lit up the room.

"Are you ready?" he said motioning to the door.

"Guess so," replied Grace.

They slowly opened the door back into the television room in the Fizzy and Busy Club. It was surprisingly noisy.

But despite the noise, the same two youngsters who had been watching television were back watching. They were laid on the fat cushions watching the television screen, both google eyed. Some unknown children's show was blaring out tunes to memorize the ABC's, while cartoon figures flew through the sky behind some dancing polar bears.

Grace and Sam headed into the other room. In this larger activity room, children were being reunited with their parents. As the various small stunned looking children were gradually matched up with their parents, their rather sad looking expressions changed to happy ones. There was a lot of noise and commotion as the families left.

Grace and Sam spotted their Mom and Dad at the other end of the room chatting to Busy, who was looking hassled checking the children in and out getting the appropriate signatures of leaving families.

Grace wondered if he was panicking as he did not know where they were. Sam was not so worried he was convinced that neither Fizzy or Busy were aware that they had left. Grace did think she saw a look of relief on Busy's face though, when Mom and Dad spotted them both across the room and waved at them smiling.

Grace and Sam rushed over hugging them. Despite all the adventures, it was a relief to be back as a family. Mom and Dad smiled and signed the check-out sheet, slightly confused as to why there was a cross there already. But soon enough, they left and got into the elevator.

Mom was babbling like she does when she has had a fun time. She told them how wonderful the countryside had been. The field of dandelions they had passed, the elegant swallows diving in and out of the houses and the beautiful vineyards.

Sam gulped at the mention of swallows. Grace smiled at him.

Mom stopped, realizing she had been talking about their day a lot.

"Did you have fun?" she asked, concerned.

"Yes," Grace exclaimed without hesitation.

"Fantastic day," agreed Sam hastily.

Mom and Dad looked relieved but slightly confused.

Mom bent down and reached for Grace's necklace.

"Look at this Dad," she said "A cool craft. Oh, look, Sam has one too."

She compared the two small pendants. "Is this made of wool?" she observed. "It must have taken you ages. What a wonderful idea. You must have used tiny needles. What does it say?"

Grace and Sam realized she was talking about the knitted medals Aunt V. had made them. The string had stretched but the medal had not grown to full size.

Sam examined it. "It says HERO," Sam explained. "We helped some of the little ones today." He had added the last part to avoid any more questions but technically it was not a lie. The Pearlball team had been helped and they were 'little' compared to them. At least before the portal.

"Cool," said Dad. He hesitated, "Ermm, do you maybe want to go back again tomorrow? Mom and I would like to do the shore trip to the ancient Roman ruins."

Sam and Grace had to contain their excitement.

"YES," they said together at the same time.

Mom and Dad looked at each other, more than a little surprised. They had been discussing this on the coach on the way home and had been sure that Grace and Sam would need lots of persuading and maybe some bribery to go back to the Kids Club again.

"Great," Dad said after a moment of stunned silence.

At that moment the elevator stopped and they piled out into the gangway.

"Did you get taller?" Dad asked Grace as he watched her get out of the elevator.

Joel was there in the gangway with his laundry cart and cleaning supplies.

"How are you?" he asked politely as they walked by.

"We are just great," answered Mom, still a little stunned by the children's eager response to return to the club tomorrow. "How are you?"

"Oh I am.... Excellent." Joel replied with his trademark smile. He winked at Grace and Sam as their parents turned to open the door to their cabin.

"Tomorrow," Sam mouthed to Joel.

Joel grinned ear to ear giving him a silent thumbs up.

"I have no idea who is going to get the top bunk tonight," Mom observed as she closed the door to get ready for dinner.

Grace and Sam looked at the towels beautifully placed on the bunk beds and smiled to themselves. The towels were in the shape of a Unicorn.

THE END - until the next time.

The Glossary

The Airflush - Geeko's invention which takes travelers from the **Gloss Room** to the **Muffle**. It has been adapted to make Reynaldo and Joel (and Grace and Sam) shrink to **Magical Folk** size so they can join in the adventures.

Aunt V. - **Gecko's** Aunt Veronica. She is friends with **Pixel's** mother and volunteers at the entrance to the **Enchanted Lodge**. She manages guests entry and exit and loves the color purple, meeting magical folk, knitting and new electronic gadgets. She is known to everyone as Aunt V.

Brilldom - the cruise ship.

The Centrifugal Porthole (CFP) or Portal - the entrance/exit to the cruise ship. Leads to the **GMSC**. It uses centrifugal force to open the hole and send people to **the Enchanted Lodge**

Chitin - delicate gleam on **fairy folk's** wings.

Coalition Security Squad- the protection service made up mostly of trolls but also witches, wizards, wolves, owls and specially trained dragons which protects the **Enchanted Alliance and Magical Folk** by providing security at **Muffles**.

Concealment - the skill used in **Pearlball** to hide yourself using colors in the background.

Electrophon - a special device on the **Magigad 3000** to help detect details. Used in the **Spy App** and **Super Ear App**.

The Enchanted Alliance – elected **Magical Folk** who govern the Magical world. They are a coalition of different Magical people working together to make decisions and keep the Magical World safe.

The Enchanted Lodge –the **Muffle** for this port where **Magical Folk** can rest, get their **Trackle** and plan their trip.

Fairy Folk - members of the **Magical Folk** who have wings. This includes fairies, pixies and elves.

Fizzy and Busy Club - the Children's Club on the **Brilldom** run by Fizzy and Busy and the location of the beginning of Grace and Sam's adventure.

Geeko - a twenty-three year old gnome who loves to engineer, he travels on the **Brilldom** to the **Muffles** on route and invents and maintains ways to exit and enter safely. Aunt V.'s nephew.

Gloss Room - Glass Moss Room (GMR) - the room at the end of the Glass Moss Slide Chute.

Glosser - Glass Moss Slide Chute (GMSC) this is the chute from the **Brilldom** ship's laundry room to the **Airflush,** which in turn leads to the **Magical Folk Local (MFL)**.

The International Tooth Depot – a secret place at each port where tooth fairies can drop off their teeth. Only tooth fairies can enter.

Joel - friend and roommate of **Reynaldo** who works on the **Brilldom** as a room concierge and steward on the days in port he likes to explore the **Magical World** with his friends **Geeko** and **Pixel**. Hobbies include towel origami and travel.

Magigad 3000 – the name of the gadget that Sam owns. It has lots of different modes including a camera, flashlight, navigation system and games. It has updated apps such as the **Spy App** and **Super Ear App**. These Apps use the **Electrophon.**

Magical Folk - term used to describe all animals and folk with magical abilities, who use their abilities for good not evil.

Magical Folk College (MFC) - the college where Aunt V. and Pixel's mother met for special courses in advanced magic and technology.

Magical Folk Local (Muffle)- the lodge or hotel or entertainment center at each port for magical folk to rest, trade or pick up their **Trackle.** In this location the **Muffle** is the **Enchanted Lodge.**

Magical World - the name given to the world in which Magical Folk coexist.

Pearlball - the most popular game in the magical world. There are rules to ensure that the team is made up of all types of different magical folk, not just one type. This makes the team inclusive and use good teamwork to coordinate and work together despite different abilities and skills. The idea is to throw the pearlball the most times into oyster shells on the opposite team's side. The oyster shells open and close at different speeds to make the task harder. Skills used are flight, speed, accuracy, timing and **concealment**.

Pearlball Tournament - a competition played once a year. **Pearlball** teams from each country compete.

Pixel - a nineteen year old fairy, who works as a tooth fairy on the **Brilldom**. In her spare time she likes to perform acrobatics and explore with her friends **Geeko**, **Joel** and **Reynaldo**.

The Portal - Geeko's invention, which takes the magical travelers down from the moss room to the port of entry, using **Glosser** and the **Airflush**.

Reynaldo - works as a cook, waiter and server on the **Brilldom**. Hobbies include gaming, baking and traveling with his friends **Joel**, **Geeko** and **Pixel**.

Spy App - a controversial app used on the **Magigad 3000** which enables the user to spy on others by using the **Electrophon**.

Super Ear App - an app used on the **Magigad 3000** which enables the user to have super hearing by using the **Electrophon**.

Sudoku Stone 5000 - new trendy game playing device which Pixel's mother gifts to Aunt V.

Trackle – a GPS type device, which is given to all **Magical Folk** to help them locate safe places to hide from Humans, especially **Weavers**. It can also summon friendly animals and birds to help them travel safely around.

The Animal Kingdom Trackle App - a mutual assistance app, on the **Trackle** which enables friendly animals, reptiles and insects registered by the **Magical Folk** to help each other.

The Weavers- evil humans, who are trying to capture fairies in order to find out the secret of staying young and to make money.

Volcanite Zone – where Magical folk can sign up for adventures.

Printed in Great Britain
by Amazon

32165505R00126